"Have I met with your approval, my Lord?"

"You please me," Lazarus said.

He approached Agnes, and he heard her breath catch in her throat, saw her pulse quicken in her neck. "Now you must only put on a convincing performance as a woman who is madly in love with me."

"I would like to eviscerate you with my teeth presently, so it will be a challenge."

And in spite of himself, he felt a kick of lust hit hard right in his stomach. He would like very much to have her use her teeth on him. And he would use his own on her in return.

He didn't know where these thoughts were coming from. These aberrations. He was not a man who was controlled by his appetites. They were an appetite like any other, and when he felt the need, he indulged them. But that was it. Right now, his desire for her was intruding. In ways he did not appreciate or accept.

D0037052

The Heirs of Liri

Two royal brothers, but only one throne...

When King Alexius de Prospero ascended to the throne of Liri, he proudly took on the role. But marrying off gorgeous Tinley Markham is his biggest royal test, especially when their chemistry proves impossible to ignore...

Wild Prince Lazarus plans to rise from the shadows and claim back his rightful throne. But as the days go on, his convenient fiancée, Agnes, may prove a tempting distraction as he starts seeing her in a totally new light!

Read Alexius and Tinley's story in
His Majesty's Forbidden Temptation
Available now!

And read Lazarus and Agnes's story in
A Bride for the Lost King
Available now!

Maisey Yates

A BRIDE FOR THE LOST KING

HARLEQUIN
PRESENTS

Recycling programs
for this product may
not exist in your area.

ISBN-13: 978-1-335-56788-8

A Bride for the Lost King

Harlequin Enterprises ULC
22 Adelaide St. West, 40th Floor
Toronto, Ontario M5H 4E3, Canada
www.Harlequin.com

Printed in U.S.A.

Maisey Yates is a *New York Times* bestselling author of over one hundred romance novels. Whether she's writing strong, hardworking cowboys, dissolute princes or multigenerational family stories, she loves getting lost in fictional worlds. An avid knitter with a dangerous yarn addiction and an aversion to housework, Maisey lives with her husband and three kids in rural Oregon. Check out her website, maiseyyates.com.

Books by Maisey Yates

Harlequin Presents

His Forbidden Pregnant Princess
Crowned for My Royal Baby

Once Upon a Seduction...

The Prince's Captive Virgin
The Prince's Stolen Virgin
The Italian's Pregnant Prisoner
The Queen's Baby Scandal
Crowning His Convenient Princess

The Heirs of Liri

His Majesty's Forbidden Temptation

Visit the Author Profile page
at Harlequin.com for more titles.

For Henry Cavill, in *The Witcher*, who really made me think a lot about the virtues of sword fighting.

CHAPTER ONE

"WHICH SWORD SHALL I take with me to meet your brother, Highness?" Agnes examined her wall of weapons critically.

She was the sworn protector of Lazarus, King of the secret kingdom at the center of the Dark Wood, in the country of Liri. A fairy tale, she would have said, something out of a picture book, until she had been brought to see it with her own eyes.

A country within a country, comprised of a village that looked as if it were part of another time, and a palace that was set deep within a mountain.

Of course, there were modern conveniences, even if hidden. Access to internet via fiber-optic cables, hot water and toaster pastries—which were her favorite.

The people in the wood were safe, kept so by the legends that surrounded it.

And outside was Liri.

Liri, ruled by King Alexius, Lazarus's brother.

The brother he'd been separated from when he'd wandered into the woods as a boy and been half savaged by wolves, saved by Agamemnon, the ruler of the woods at the time.

In Lazarus he'd seen greatness. In him, he'd seen the salvation of his people, occupied and kept down by the Lirians, before they were driven to the brink of extinction.

As far as all the world knew, their kingdom did not exist.

And until a few weeks ago, the world had not known Lazarus existed.

He had traveled freely, under an assumed name, and no one had ever suspected he was the long-lost prince thought long-ago dead.

But Lazarus had been planning revenge against his family for years. In fact, he had been intent on stealing his brother's fiancée. Literally stealing her. Right from the woods, until an interaction between the two of them had stayed his hand.

He had promised the previous leader, Agamemnon, that he would avenge the people. For as she was sworn to Lazarus, so was he to the previous leader of the people. He had promised that he would return their people to their rightful place on the throne. For it was not Lazarus and Alex's family who held that right, but the people of the trees. They had been killed. They had been weakened and shunted off into the forest, but they had not diminished. No, there they had grown. She was not of them. Not by blood. But it didn't matter. Not to them. It was the outcasts that they took. Those who were left to their own devices. Those who were in need.

Like her.

"You shall not be bringing a sword, Agnes."

When Lazarus made a pronouncement, in that deep voice like velvet dipped in gold, she never argued.

She liked the way he said her name. *Ah-nes*. As if she were something exotic and not something neighboring an agate. Which was how she always thought of her name.

But she did *not* like what he'd just said.

"I cannot travel without a sword, Highness, for it is my sworn duty to protect you. A blood oath bonds us." She tilted her chin upward, meeting his gaze.

Lazarus was tall, over six-five, with the sculpted face of an avenging angel. At least in part. It was his scars—deep, lashing and cruel, covering half of that face—that gave him the manner of devil. Dark eyes, hard as obsidian, and a mouth that turned over into cruel with the slightest curve. He was not a man who looked as if he needed protection.

But in her world, in *their* world, in the wood, when a person was saved from death, they swore fealty to their savior. As she had done to Lazarus when she was just sixteen, and in the eight years since.

They were bonded by something deeper than blood. He had risked his life to save hers. Her blood, her very breath, belonged to him.

Though she needed a sword if she were to be effective.

"Bringing a sword into the palace is an act of war, Agnes," he said, as if she did not know.

"It is an act of caution. You do not know your brother well."

Agnes could not deny that she felt a slight bit of relief hearing him speak in a way that seemed to indicate he would not be waging war.

His aim had shifted since the time he had decided to leave the forest and seek his revenge on Alexius. That first day, that meeting, she had been hiding in the woods. In the darkness with her sword ready to be drawn. But no fighting had ensued. They had simply talked. And in the times since, Lazarus had been opaque. Regarding his plans to return to the kingdom of his heart, of his blood, and regarding his intent when it came to his brother, Alexius.

If she were a woman who believed she could know the mysteries of a man like Alexius, she might have taken his connecting with his brother at face value.

But she was not. So, she did not.

"Well, I suppose a dagger…"

"We do not come to make *open* war," he continued. "Revenge must be accomplished quietly."

She stopped, the hair on the back of her neck standing on end. "I thought you were through with revenge."

"Did I say so?"

"No, but you…you spoke to him. You advised him to stay on with…with Tinley. To love her. I heard you."

"It is true," he said, "I did. And it softened what I am willing to consider. But he will still have a difficult choice to make. Reconciliation. And recognition of me as King. Or…"

"King?"

"Over Liri and the wood. To give our people that which they've been denied."

"And why didn't you tell me this sooner?"

"My plans are not for you to know, little one."

"I wish you wouldn't call me that. I could cut down any man where he stands, whether he was anticipating the attack or not. Small though I may be, I am deadly."

"To be certain," he said. "But little all the same. And while your skill with a sword is greatly appreciated, Agnes, it is not what I need of you at this time."

"What is it you do need?"

"You've sworn your loyalty to me. Whatever

my commandment, you shall fulfill, is that not the way?"

"Whatever your command," she confirmed. "My life is yours." And she meant it, from the deepest part of her soul.

"Good. You are not coming as my shield maiden."

She blinked, feeling off-balance. "Then what am I? If not your protector, then what am I?"

"You will be coming as my fiancée."

Agnes was stunned. She was… Well, she was *barely* a woman, in all actuality. She had been trained to follow the way of the sword. The way of battle. Her body was honed into one of ruthless athleticism, her instincts sharpened by years of training. Training that she had taken at Lazarus's own hand. She did not know feminine ways. And often felt outside of the groups of brightly dressed women in their kingdom.

But then, she was an outsider.

Saved by Lazarus. Brought here.

He had incapacitated the five men surrounding her with ruthless brutality and speed. And while she had been grateful, she had also been left standing there alone.

Except for him.

He was dressed nicely, black pants and a crisp white shirt that was still somehow clean in spite of what had occurred. His clothing was improbably civilized. The man himself had the look of a bar-

barian. Black hair cut to ruthless precision, broad shoulders. His sleeves were pushed up past his elbows, revealing well-muscled forearms.

He was terrifying and beautiful. A savior and a potential danger.

And her father was dead. And even though her immediate threat had been dispatched, the danger out there in the world for a sixteen-year-old girl who knew nothing of life, who knew nothing other than what her con man father had taught her… There was nothing good to be had. She had known of a great many things she could do to survive, but she was loath to do any of them.

And so, when the mighty warrior had turned to leave, she had followed.

"Where are you going?" she asked.

He didn't spare her a glance. "Back to my kingdom. At least, at some point today, I will be."

"Can I go with you?"

He had stopped. Then turned, regarding her with seriousness. And in that moment it had struck her that he was the most beautiful man she had ever seen. Beautiful and terrifying.

All at once.

"In my country there is a tradition. If one saves the life of another, that person swears that life to them. Your service. Is that the life you want?"

"Who talks like that?" she asked.

"I do." His accent was heavy, but beautiful.

"Are you a King of some kind?"

His lips curved. "Of some kind."

And she realized that she could be stepping out of one danger and into another entirely. But he had saved her life, and he didn't have to. So at the very least, he must not intend to kill her. As for the rest… Well, she could cope.

And it had turned out that Lazarus was all that he claimed to be. Especially when it came to his expectations for her. When it came to his adherence to tradition. He had helped her become a warrior, an option that she had not thought existed for a woman such as her. And so she had sworn her loyalty to him. To their country. She had changed her every thought and expectation about her future, all for him.

"Your fiancée," she said, feeling very much like she had reached the end of her loyalty in that moment. For that was… An impossibility. Something she knew was an impossibility. He was a King. She was a no one. From the streets of nowhere in particular. America originally, but then Italy, France, anywhere her father could run a scam. A girl who spoke bits and pieces of different languages but had never really owned any of them. Had never sworn allegiance to any one country, to any one leader. Until now. Until him.

And she had sworn with all of herself to protect him, because she could never be anything more.

It was foolish.

He was more than a man. He was something more like a god. And he was untouchable. Especially for her. She didn't know his age. It had never seemed to matter. It just wasn't relevant. For he was more than she was. More than she ever could be.

Untouchable. Remote and unreachable.

"I'm sorry," she said. "I must've misunderstood."

"I think we both know you did not. Your senses are finely honed, thanks to my training."

"Yes. All glory to you," she said, barely able to keep the sarcasm from her tone. She did mean that. Typically.

"And so, you see, this is what must occur."

"No, I am afraid I do not see."

"You are my right hand, Agnes. And have been these many years. This is my sworn duty to this country. To lay claim to the throne."

Yes, she was his right hand. A tool. A weapon. A shield.

She was not a woman. Not to him.

And if Agnes had found it to be incredibly painful, it was only her problem. No one could solve it for her. And it was one she would simply have to bear. She had borne a great many disappointments in her life.

What was one more?

She loved him. With all that she was. Her soul, her heart, her sword. Her body.

She had discovered desire sparring with him, watching the play of his muscles as he moved. She had become acquainted with what it meant to be a woman.

He lit up the most womanly places in her, enflamed fantasies that she had not ever thought she'd entertained.

He did not see her as a woman, however, and she had accepted that.

She was his Agnes, and whatever she was, she was at least singular.

If she could never have him as a woman did a man, she would take that. She mattered. She was not like the endless parade of curvy beauties who had his attention for a night.

What she had was better.

She cared for him though, a great deal, even if she had accepted he would not be hers.

She had assumed then, wrongly, that Lazarus had decided on a path of forgiveness. And it occurred to her now that she didn't actually know what her King sought to do.

"It is not war. But a reckoning. A reclamation. Sad, indeed, that there may be bloodshed. Blood which I share."

Agnes thought of King Alexius's lovely bride-to-be. With her beautiful red hair. The future Queen Tinley. She was truly a lovely girl. And Agnes did not like the thought of something evil befalling her.

Agnes had only seen her once. From her position hiding in the forest. But Agnes had seen enough.

"You will spare Tinley."

"I will spare him if he will give in to what I ask. What I demand. But it is rare that a King will give up his kingdom."

"But you do not think the kingdom rightly belongs to him."

"It was stolen. By my family. By my bloodline. *Our* bloodline. And it is up to me to make it right. I have sworn my loyalty here. Not to them. But here. To these people. It must be fulfilled. Those promises. That loyalty. If Alex wishes to make his reparation I do not see the point in taking anything by force. But if he does not…"

"I do understand," she said. "But it seems that there could be…"

"This is not a con, Agnes. There is no negotiation to be made. No side alleys that one can take." Her cheeks stung with heat.

And shame.

"I did not mean it in that way," she said.

Her father had been a con artist; she was not.

"I know you did not. I'm simply pointing out that we are made from different molds, you and I."

"I am made from the mold that you forged me in," she said, tilting her chin up. "And I do wish that you would allow me to bring a sword."

"As I said, we are not making open war."

"But we *are* making war."

The way that his mouth shifted seemed to confirm that, whether he would say it or not.

"You will be provided with a wardrobe. From Paris."

"What do I care of Paris?" she asked. "I've seen it."

"You've seen alleyways. It is not the same."

It was not like Lazarus to take pains to remind her where she had come from. He was not usually cool. But it didn't matter. It didn't matter what he said, when or how. Her loyalty was sworn. Her fate was set. Whether she agreed or not, it made no matter. Whether she wanted to or not, it had no bearing. She was Agnes, with no family name. Agnes of the Dark Wood. And nothing more.

Agnes, Shield Maiden of Lazarus.

And thus she would remain.

"Whatever you require of me," she said. "This I shall do."

"Then you shall come with me now," he said. "To Paris."

CHAPTER TWO

MONEY DIDN'T MATTER in the Dark Wood. But Lazarus himself knew how to wield it to his advantage, knew exactly how to slide into the moneyed circles that he sometimes must inhabit.

Agamemnon had taught him that a leader—even a leader who operated in secret—could not afford to be ignorant of the world. He had helped him create a background that would give him the necessary paperwork to travel. To exist. He had taught him about money, investments, which Lazarus had taken to easily. He had taken the money held by his people and increased it tenfold.

He moved seamlessly between the borders of the wood and other parts of Europe, where he slid off the mantle of guardian of the forest and put on a suit.

He did not take Agnes with him on such sojourns, not usually. Though, it was how he had found her in the first place. But it was the only time they had traveled in this manner together. She never liked it.

She didn't like to let him out of her sight.

She was dedicated, his warrior, though he knew that he didn't actually require her presence in order to keep himself safe. No, it was more to do with her. With protecting her, though he knew that she would bristle at the assertion.

Poor Agnes.

But this… This was the way in which she could prove useful. For Alexius desired the two of them to have a relationship—one like brothers. And if Lazarus had not been hardened by his years, by the early loss of his family. A family who had not even searched for him. Then he might feel guilt that he had no such intent.

They had met only twice since he had first revealed himself to Alexius, with Alexius inviting him to come and stay before his wedding to Tinley. He'd had a few weeks to consider that and decide his next move.

The presence of a fiancée on his arm would soften Lazarus's appearance.

Since his own face would not do it.

He had come to terms with his scars long ago. In the wood it was a symbol of survival. Of his strength.

Out in the world sometimes he was greeted with terrified stares.

But there were many women who worshipped those scars. Who found them dangerous and very, very appealing.

And so he had learned to use them.

As he would use Agnes. To make himself seem human.

Not that Agnes was soft. She was fierce and sharp, and much like traveling with a live possum. She was comically small but muscled from her years of training. She was fast, and she was quick in mind and movement.

And currently, she was seated on the floor of his private jet, wearing her typical uniform of baggy linen pants and an equally loose-cut top. Her knees were pulled up to her chest, her black hair pulled up into a high ponytail. Her dark eyes glittered in distaste. She was a woman with no country, she had said it often, until she had come to live in his. His hidden country at the center of another. And she was also a woman whose heritage was impossible to divine. Her eyes were catlike and tilted upward, her mouth full, her skin a cinnamon color.

She was pretty. Though, he did not often ponder her appearance.

It was relevant now only because her beauty made her a believable choice as fiancée.

"It would not harm you to come and sit on the furniture."

She looked up at him. "I've no need."

"You are not a feral animal, and it does not benefit either of us for you to behave as such."

She frowned. "Does it benefit a warrior to grow soft?"

"You are not needed in that capacity."

"I resent it."

"Do you? What I require is someone I can trust. Absolutely. That, I assumed I could do with you. No one knows of my plans. It is not safe. Can I not trust you?"

She scrambled to her feet. "You can trust me. With your life."

"And so I thought. This is simply another kind of mission."

She wrinkled her nose, then with some reluctance came to sit at the far end of a couch with a great distance between her and the chair in which he sat.

Funny creature. Was she so thrown off by his request for her to fulfill this new role?

Well. He supposed she was so unaccustomed to this kind of softness. They enjoyed the simple life in the wood.

She seemed happy there, though she did not seem to have friends. But then, neither did he. He felt that he and Agnes were of the same mind in many ways. They kept to themselves. They cared more about their disciplines. About their responsibilities.

Neither of them was frivolous.

And yet he would have to engage in some frivolousness now. The truth was, the news of his resurrection from the dead had been internationally recognized, and he was not used to such a thing.

He was known in business circles, and had been for some time, but he did not court the spotlight. For clear reasons.

But that had changed, and it meant that this engagement needed to occur on the same stage. Otherwise, it would not look real. His brother would not believe that he took a woman without showering her in gifts. Without a trip to Paris. At least, that was not the sort of man he wished the world to believe he was.

He would have to marry, it was true. He would have to have an heir. But, in the woods, courtship rituals were much different. Vows were spoken between the lovers, the world was not involved. It seemed to him a fine way to conduct courtship. And yet, it was not the way of the outside world. Whether he agreed with it or not, he could understand it.

When the plane touched down in Paris, there was a car waiting for them. All of their items were loaded into it, and Agnes walked with her head down, her expression determined.

"Where have you acquired all these things?" she said, when they were on the road. He wondered if she was trying to act unimpressed with the city around them. Though, as she had said, she had been here before.

"Surely you must know that I have taken the riches of our kingdom and multiplied them."

"Yes," she said. "Though, I confess I did not realize it was… Riches in the sense of what exists out in this world."

Value in the wood came from what was useful, and what was beautiful. The time and effort and talent put into creating. It was different, but they could not thrive without bringing in amenities from the outside world. It was simply not possible. And so, money was necessary.

And he had made it abundant. His first step in securing a better, safer future for his adopted people.

"Of course it is," he said. "I'm a practical man above all else, Agnes."

"Well. I know. But I find the world out here to be *impractical*. You forget that I used to live in it. For longer than you did."

He looked at her for a long moment. He didn't forget much, but he supposed he did forget that on occasion.

"True. You are a woman of this world."

"I'm not," she said, shaking her head. "I have released my hold on it. There was never going to be anything for me out here."

She looked out the car window.

"You're resourceful," he said.

"It's true," she said. She turned to look at him, her dark gaze bold and direct. "Being here though, is a stark reminder of what I would have become. I was prepared to do what I had to do. But prior to your teaching me to fight, prior to your teaching me to defend myself, I had accepted that the only option would be eventually to sell my body. I did not wish to do it."

The idea of Agnes being forced to sell her warrior's body, being forced to tear pieces off her strong, proud soul stirred anger in his blood. "This world is a scourge," he said.

Lazarus's infusion of money had brought technology, had given them the means to import goods used by their small nation that numbered no more than one thousand.

But modernity brought its own vices, as well as its virtues. Their world was not perfect.

But it was a small community, and when there was an injustice it was corrected, and quickly. Taking advantage of anyone poor was not permitted. And when there were resources to be shared around, no one was left without food. They shared among themselves. Their economy existed largely as one rooted in trade. And those who were weak were cared for.

"You get no argument from me. I much prefer to wield a blade."

The car carried them directly to the department store they would be shopping from, and they were led into a private room at the very top of an exclusive elevator.

The room was all brightly lit, with dark wood and walls of mirrors. There was already a slim dress rack with several selections on it. Everything prepared for their arrival, as he had commanded.

A very slim woman dressed all in black appeared a moment later.

"This is she?" she asked.

"Yes," Lazarus said, not bothering to answer in French or English. He used Lirian, and the woman would figure it out.

Agnes, on the other hand, slipped easily into French. The woman took Agnes into the dressing room, and a moment later shrieked.

She came out, speaking English to Lazarus. "Your creature has a knife on her person."

"I could not come unarmed!" The woman walked out from the curtain, and Agnes poked her head out behind her. "I will not use it on you."

Lazarus waved a hand. "She is not a creature. She is a warrior. And my fiancée. And you will relay none of the information about the knife, but will tell whoever asks you that she is lovely, and loved beyond all women. Or there will be no payment made to you, do you understand?"

The woman's cheeks went red. "Understood, Your Highness."

She disappeared again, and there was a rustling sound, and a moment later, Agnes was forced from behind the curtain.

Agnes felt foolish. She had never worn anything like this. Usually, when she had been with her father, she had been dressed to look younger. Or to look like a boy. Either to be pitiful, or to be discreet. But she had never worn anything like this. The dress was red, bold, clinging to her body in such a way that she felt naked. Naked, standing before Lazarus, which made her feel like she was melting, possibly like she was on fire.

"It is unseemly," she said, turning and walking back behind the curtains and closing them definitively. She could nearly feel the indignation of the woman who had helped her dress, even from the other side of the curtains.

She looked in the mirror, glad to be shielded from Lazarus's all too keen gaze.

She didn't recognize the woman that she saw standing there. Who looked surprisingly thin and shapely all at once, and whose body seemed to be firmly entrenched in this world, while her hair remained wild and part of another place and time. And then suddenly, the curtains parted, and he was there.

"This is hardly the loyalty you profess to bear, Agnes."

"I do not recall wearing gowns to be part of my training."

"Whatever my order." He looked at her, hard, and she realized she was… Defying him. Something she had never done.

Lazarus was a strong man, a strong leader, and he had no issues with people speaking their minds to him, and Agnes often shared her thoughts. But that was not the same as direct defiance.

But maybe it was being here.

In Paris.

Where her old life had ended and her new life had begun.

It had her on edge.

He had her on edge.

She turned to him. "I do not like it."

She felt more than naked before his burning gaze. She felt something else entirely, and she did not care for it in the least.

"Agnes," he said, his words as hard as his stare. "You will do this."

"I hardly think that I need trot out in front of you like a fashion model."

"I've no use for fashion models," he said. His gaze was assessing. "It is not the fashion that I care for, but rather whether or not you play the part well."

"Am I not looking the part?"

"We will see if that is so once your hair is dealt with." He snapped his fingers. "On to the next garment."

Then the woman was back, the curtains closed again, and Agnes was peeled out of the dress, and the second was practically painted on over her body. It was green, and the fabric draped in places, and it made her look even curvier than the first, though it wasn't quite as tight. The top draped down low, exposing the sides of her breasts.

Lazarus looked at her in that, and her skin felt scalded. Because now he was looking at her as a woman, but still not as she would like. He was seeing her as a tool, and evaluating her appearance as if that would tell him how useful a tool she was.

Far better to have him evaluate her skills with a sword than her body. For this hurt far too much.

But the indignity did not stop. After that dress, there was a gold gown, with a skirt yet more voluminous, and she didn't think she would have a hope of hiding a scabbard in the folds, and that was cheering to an extent. At least until Lazarus appraised her, with that same detached efficiency that she found exceedingly unnerving.

"We will take them all," he said. "And other supplemental pieces. You have a very fortunate figure, Agnes."

That made Agnes want to claw her scalding skin right off. "A *fortunate figure*?"

"Yes. Every style seems to suit you."

"Maybe I don't like them," she said.

"I do not care for your preferences, little one. It is mine that will be served. As I think you know."

An angry pulse beat between her thighs, and she could not reconcile it with the anger that flowed through her veins. That at least was the burden she had borne for years. This need of him. A need she had accepted could become nothing.

And yet also, beneath that was loyalty. Loyalty she could not escape or deny. She had sworn her life to him. When she had sworn her allegiance to their nation. It was the first time she had ever been part of anything. Anything other than that accident of birth. Which was nothing true or real. Her father had not been a real father to her. He had loyalty to nothing but himself. And Agnes prized her word above all else, because when she had been brought into Lazarus's life, she had been made a new creation. A woman who knew the keenest of loyalties. A woman who believed in truth. A woman who prized honesty. A woman who made it her mission, every day, to find her place in this broad world. She had made herself a woman of truth.

Her father would have turned her into the same sort of scammer con artist that he was. Seeking only her own comfort, seeking only her own pleasure.

She would have to remember that even now, that her own feelings were not what mattered. For that was a philosophy that carried you only to the depths of extreme selfishness, and then on to ruin. And she should know.

Her father had used her as a pawn, and he would've signed her death warrant if not for Lazarus.

"As you will it," she responded.

And that was how she found herself being bundled back into a car, feeling edgy and angry. But they did not go back toward the airport.

"What are we doing?" she asked.

"We are to make our debut as a couple."

"What is all this?" she asked. "Debuts and shows for the press. Lazarus, if you're on a mission of blood, how does raising your profile in the world help you at all?"

"It's not that simple. And, as I said, it is not my goal to kill my brother. Rather I would like that he willingly step aside."

"And what is this game?"

It was the deceit that truly got to her. And it was recognizing that Lazarus felt a sense of honor here, but that he was…

She respected him, so much, and knew he was a good man, but she did wonder if he could always see clearly.

How could you when your soul was shrouded in darkness?

"I must put him at ease."

She swallowed hard, conscience pricking at her eyes. She understood where Lazarus was coming from. She knew him better than she knew any other person on the planet. He was her mentor. He was... Well, he was everything.

They drove until they arrived at a lovely building, with the Eiffel Tower at its back. And just then she had a feeling that he was right, and she had not ever truly seen Paris before. He got out of the car, and opened the door for her, taking her arm and ushering her into a building that she was very truly not dressed for. But no one gave them a second glance, everyone committed to being the center of their own universe in this beautiful space filled with ancient stone, marble and gilded edges.

They went to an elevator that opened with the touch of Lazarus's hand, and it went straight to the very top of the building, the doors opening inside a brilliantly appointed penthouse.

The views of the city were sweeping, and the entire wall of windows in this unexpectedly modern space stole the attention from the rest of the interior. For it was Paris that was the true decor. The Arc de Triomphe, the Eiffel Tower, the Seine running through the lovely brick streets, and she could see artists with their canvases set up, ready to paint the world as they saw it, fashion mavens wandering the streets in long coats and large sunglasses, with brilliantly bored expressions.

It was all there, and all very French. And it took her a moment to realize that the inside was no less chic. It was modern. Cement floors and counter-tops, black details and chrome lines.

"Did you choose this?" she asked.

If so, it was an insight into him that she never had before. Who he was away from the wood, away from his castle made of rock and stone.

"No. I had an employee select something suitable. Others of my people will be here for you soon."

He was not wrong, as a moment later, a man and two women appeared, and she found herself being nearly bodily carried into a bathroom the size of an apartment she had once shared with her father. Lazarus was nowhere to be seen as she was stripped, reluctantly divested of her weapon and placed into a steaming tub of water.

She was scrubbed, she was combed, her hair was cut by one of the ruthlessly thin females, who took her mane from the middle of her back, up to the bottom of her shoulder blades in a blunt, asymmetrical line.

They put foils in her hair, and the scent of chemicals was strong. It made her eyes prickle, because it reminded her of dyeing her hair when she and her father had been running, or creating new identities.

Blond. Brown. Black. Red.

Her hair had spanned every color of the spectrum. This was different, though, as what they did didn't transform her entire head. No. Rather her black hair faded to a sort of caramel brown at the ends, and she looked grown-up in a way she never had before. And never really thought about.

Her nails were painted, and so was her face, with a thick liner making the already turned up corners of her eyes even more dramatic, and a pale blush staining her high cheeks, along with a gloss on her mouth.

And then there were clothes. Not the gowns that she had tried on earlier, but a knee-length, cashmere skirt in a camel color, and a pair of sky-high black shoes. A buttery soft gray sweater, and a coat that matched the skirt and nearly touched the ground.

She didn't recognize herself. But one thing she did comfort herself with was the fact that the lines of the outfit did allow for weaponry.

And just like that, the team who turned her into this entirely new being vanished, never really speaking to her, never really acting like she was anything more than a life-size doll. The stranger in the mirror was disquieting. Because though it was certainly something more than what had happened when she had changed identities when she and her father had changed locations, it still reminded her of that time.

That shape-shifting that had been born out of a necessity to... To live.

And now, even as she was being true to Lazarus, she was part of a lie.

But you are loyal to him. You are true to him.

You are still Agnes of the forest.

And not Agnes of lies.

She looked at herself again and felt a strange sense of…pride. She looked soft. She felt beautiful.

Like a woman.

She rejected that. Hard.

She took a breath, and walked over to her suitcase, where she had concealed a sword.

Is this not a lie?

She did not listen to that scathing tone in her voice. She didn't have the time for it. Nor the patience. And she took a rather substantial-size dagger out of the bag, and lifted her sweatshirt, undoing her skirt before strapping it ruthlessly beneath her clothes, and then she went out into the living area to await her orders. But she was not prepared for what awaited her there. For there was Lazarus, but as she'd not seen him. Wearing a superbly cut black suit, and a long black coat. His black hair was pushed back off of his face, showing the sharpness of his cheekbones, the extreme perfection of his features.

And for the first time, she fully appreciated who she was looking at. He was Lazarus, a prince of Liri.

A man who should've grown up in splendor, in a palace, had he not been left to his own devices in the woods. Had he not been taken in by the people of the forest.

And for the first time, she wondered that he was not more angry at them. For they had taken him from a life of luxury, and brought him into a hard, hard world.

And though it was one that she personally loved, her own destiny had not been a palace, but death at the hands of the men who had killed her father. She would have died in a French alley if not for Lazarus and the people of the wood.

But Lazarus would have been a prince. Lazarus would've had a family. A mother and father.

He would have been beautiful, not scarred.

Though his scars were beautiful to her.

They represented all he'd suffered. And her own salvation as a result.

"Come, Agnes," he said, extending his hand. "For we have dinner reservations."

CHAPTER THREE

HE HAD NOT anticipated just how beautiful he would find her. He had never looked at her and seen a woman.

She was a creature that he had rescued, and for the better, as she had been such a small, soft thing when he had first discovered her.

Not much more than sixteen and cowering in terror in an alley, about to be killed. But likely not before she endured other travesties.

Her father had already been gone, his blood spilled on the pavement.

He would not allow the same fate to befall her. And he had known that. He had also known in that moment that they were bonded.

It had been the same for him.

When he had been a boy, and he had wandered off into the woods from a palace he could now no longer remember, he had been backed into a corner by wolves. Flat against the side of a cliff, those evil beasts snarling at him.

And in a breath, they had fallen on him. His skin torn away from his flesh.

Being devoured even while he screamed.

He had waited for death. Hoped for it. Even as a small child.

But then Agamemnon had come.

Agamemnon of the Wood.

He had taken Lazarus, bleeding and broken, back to the village. Had given him rest and medical attention.

He had told him going home was not safe at first. And indeed, at first, he had lacked the strength.

Agamemnon had explained if he were to ever show his face out of the wood, their people would be destroyed. And Lazarus, young though he was, had asked why.

And what he had learned was the hideous history of how the conquerors who had come to their land had renamed it Liri. Had pushed the original inhabitants to the outskirts. Tried to snuff out their culture.

He had said Lazarus's parents would search for him.

That they would find him and then the people of the wood would be rewarded and not harmed.

They had never come.

Scouts had watched for them. No one had ever looked.

Agamemnon had become like a father to him. It was not the same soft childhood he'd had at the palace, but the memories of it had faded soon enough.

He ran around the campfires with the other children. He was fed by the women there too. He grew strong outdoors.

Eventually, Agamemnon had introduced him to his dogs. Hulking, great beasts that helped keep the people safe.

Lazarus had looked at them and seen only wolves.

Terror had streaked through him, and his memories of pain had been too much to bear. Agamemnon had not let him run. He had been firm.

You will learn to care for them.

They will be yours.

You will overcome your fears.

I saved you, and you will swear yourself to me, Lazarus. It is the way of things. I saved your life, and it is mine.

And Lazarus had done so. And his parents still had not come.

He had grown into a man without fear, a man without pain, and his parents had not come.

But Agamemnon and his adopted people had been enough.

* * *

If it had not been for Agamemnon, he would've been consumed by those beasts. Eaten, as he had found out his brother he had never met was. The brother who had replaced him.

It had been too late to save him.

Lazarus mourned that.

He mourned the loss of that boy.

He did not mourn the loss of that life he would've had at the palace, though. Though the distinction of how heirs were chosen in Liri was important. A brother could challenge his brother for the throne. And the people could choose a new leader.

It was his great-grandfather who had sidelined his people. Who had destroyed their way of life. His blood. And when he swore allegiance to his new family, he had been clear that he would see all things put to rights.

It was his duty, sworn and solemn, to avenge them. To restore balance, and well he knew it.

It was his duty to do as was his right. To challenge the heir to the throne. To seek that which could be rightfully his. Rightfully his people's.

Yes, he had known, the moment that he had rescued Agnes, that she had consequence in his life. For was it not simply—she had come to understand later—that the person you saved must swear their allegiance to you, it was only that being entrusted with that life was incredibly weighty, and binding. For both members of the blood bond.

Just as her life was his, that responsibility held meaning. There was a purpose behind it.

The purpose behind him being saved by the people of the wood was that he might restore an entire nation to its rightful place, and Agnes was a key part of that. Deeply important to the cause.

And so, it should not surprise him at all that she was perfect to play the role.

She was elegant, a quicksilver beauty who he knew to be deadly, but what surprised him the most was that she could still be soft.

For the first time since he'd first met her, Agnes looked hesitant.

Perhaps it was because they were back in Paris. He had not fully thought about it, but it made sense that she might be… That she might be frightened. Of Paris and all that it represented. Of the memories that lurked here. He could well understand.

He was not looking forward to going back to the palace of Liri, but fear did not live inside of him. Not anymore. He had banished it when he had first touched the dogs that looked so much like the beasts that had savaged him. The lesson in that had been that a man must be stronger than pain, than weakness.

Agnes was young. A warrior, yes, but she had also been sixteen when she'd left Paris. It was possible there were memories here for her she had not yet come to terms with.

"Are you well?"

"I am as ever," she said, lifting her chin. He held his hand out to her, and she took it reluctantly.

And the moment that his skin touched hers, he felt a kick of extreme arousal. It echoed that which had roared to life in him when she'd begun to try those dresses on. Showing her body in a way that was undeniably feminine.

It was unwelcome. This was Agnes. And she was not a woman that he could use in such a fashion. She was his… His ward in many ways. His responsibility on a deep level. There were many willing, round women back in the forest who could satisfy his urges as they satisfied their own. A pleasing transaction all around. It was the way of things.

His adopted culture was open about sex. But it was something that must be kept in its place.

He was a warrior.

Female warriors were to be treated as brothers-in-arms. With Agnes being even more complicated because she was his responsibility.

His.

It was the power that he wielded over her life, the power that he had, that made it unacceptable.

She was looking very serious as they walked out of the penthouse and onto the elevator. But he did not waver. They arrived down at the lobby to the building, and he moved nearer to her, and he could feel her every muscle tighten, get twitchy.

He put his arm around her and pulled her yet more closely. And felt hard steel beneath her clothing. As soon as they were out on the street he turned his head and pressed his mouth to her ear.

"Agnes," he said. "Do you have a sword beneath your clothes?"

She did not look at him. But for the first time, her expression became sanguine. "I'm committed to my duty."

"I believe I told you no swords. And already you nearly created an international incident in the dressing room of a very nice shop. Why is it that you saw to ignore my edict and arm yourself?"

"I have sworn a duty to protect you, my Lord, and I will do so. To the best of my ability and as I see fit."

"You will do as I see fit," he said.

"I believe it is within my right to judge whether or not I believe the situation calls for added protection. And in that you do not have the right to tell me what to do."

"I have every right," he said. "I have every right to tell you exactly what you should do for me."

"I have agreed to this," she said. "Do you not think that perhaps I have a fair idea of what my function is. Even if you have replaced it entirely."

"I value you, Agnes, and I do not take our bond

lightly, but please drop this idea that I require you for protection. That you could do anything for me that I cannot do for myself."

He heard her gasp, but she swallowed it quickly, and the two of them carried on down the street.

The crowd parted for them, and Lazarus took it as his due. Royalty were given deference because of their position in society, because of the fear that people felt that they might face consequences should they fail to genuflect as expected. Or the hope that they might be rewarded should they behave in a certain manner. Lazarus did not need to be raised a prince to create a parting of the seas. It was not that he was royal, but that he was a man of consequence. A man of consequence did not need status in order to influence the crowd. He simply needed to breathe.

They continued on down the street to the restaurant, which was a building with a simple limestone facade. Exactly the sort of place that one might go if they wished to avoid the paparazzi. Lazarus did not wish to avoid the paparazzi, quite the opposite. He intended to court them. But the paparazzi were always where they felt they might not be wanted, and so it made the perfect location for such an endeavor.

They walked in, where they were known by sight, and were ushered to the finest table, in a corner of the restaurant that allowed them to see out over the room and place no one at their backs.

Neither he nor Agnes could ever bear sitting with their back to a door, or to a room of people. A wall it must be.

"Are there menus?" Agnes asked.

"A waste of time and paper. We will be served only their finest. And all of it."

Agnes, for all that she was trying to be casual, glittered with interest then.

That was one thing he appreciated about Agnes. She liked food. She liked it quite a bit.

There were certain little things that she seemed to enjoy, hearkening back to a time, he knew, when she had little.

For all that he had not grown up in a palace, Lazarus had always had plenty. Agnes, he knew, had experienced having nothing.

And when there was a feast, she ate her fill and then some.

"I do hope there is steak," she said.

Agnes was not disappointed on that score. There was steak. Marrow, cheese and bread. And a host of the desserts. And for a moment, he allowed the mission to fade into the background as he watched her enjoy all that was set before her.

And he felt… Self-congratulatory. For on this, he had kept his word, and his honor. Her life was his. In his care, and he had presented her with true finery. He had been much softer to her than Agamemnon had been to him. He had not had her sleep upon the rocks in order to earn her right to a bed by proving her strength.

She was better for having met him.

She looked up at him, her expression suddenly narrow. "And what is it you're thinking about?"

"Your good fortune," he said. "To be in my care."

The corner of her mouth went tight. "Oh, is that so?"

"Yes. Look at this food that you enjoy."

"I have *eaten* the food that I enjoy," she said. "I did not spend any time looking at it. Nor will I."

"A beast you are, Agnes. We must work on that." He had spent time in the world, it was why he had found her. How he had saved her.

It was, perhaps, one area of his responsibility where he had been remiss with her.

Agnes was in his care, and it must be acknowledged that her life with him had been… Narrow. And if that was so, it was a failing.

The concept of ownership, when it came to things, to land, was loose among their people. Yes, the King was steward of the riches of the people, but it was not the same as ownership.

Even his own life was not his possession, for it belonged to the people who saved him.

But a lifesaving bond, as the two of them had, was binding.

Agnes was the one thing that was truly his.

"I shall work on nothing but this cake," she said,

taking a large slice of chocolate cake from the dessert platter that sat on the edge of the table.

"Careful. You do look a bit feral."

"I *am* a bit feral. It is not my fault that you elected to take me to this restaurant without any forewarning. Trussed up in finery I may be, but I am what I am."

"We both know that isn't true. You have the ability to fit in wherever you go. You were raised to do so."

"I don't like that part of my life."

"When you were in Paris did you ever go to places such as this?"

"No," she said. "I did not. And I think you know that."

"A question. For I wondered if this return to Paris was one filled with memories."

"I do remember the alleyways," she said sharply. "Particularly when I nearly died in one. Why were you in Paris then?"

"Part of my education," he said. "Agamemnon never intended to keep me in the forest, wholly uncivilized. I'm only mostly uncivilized. But I have to be able to blend in with my surroundings when it is required, and it is required soon. I'm grateful for that time."

"I had no such time. But I don't want it."

She was his. His to do right by. His to protect. And now he was having thoughts about her that were not honorable. He had kept her apart from the whole world, which was not as Agamemnon had done for him later. And he was…

He could not trust his intentions toward her entirely.

He had to think about her. And her healing. About her potential.

She would fare well out here in the world. She was beautiful and smart and capable.

And he alone possessed the power to give her the chance to be all she could.

Something in him softened. "Agnes, when this is through, I will release you."

Her eyes went wide. "What does that mean?"

"You want not to be tied to me forever. I've taken care of you. And I have done a wonderful job."

"If you say so yourself."

"Do you not have skills? Can you not defend yourself? Are you not fed and clothed?"

"I am all those things," she said tartly.

"Then I have done well by you, have I not?"

"I imagine so."

"And I find my responsibility toward you is quite deep."

She shifted. "Do you?"

"A person cannot know how they wish to spend all of their time on this earth if they have not experienced different facets of life. You must experience more."

"And if I don't wish to?"

She was being stubborn, as she often was.

"It is not a matter of what you wish. It is simply a matter of what is. But you must have your education. You must have your time in the civilized world."

"Must I?" she said.

"Yes. So in the end, I will allow you the same freedom that was given to me."

"Catch and release," she said, quite meanly as she took a bite of her cake.

"Yes. And you may not wish it, because you are attached to the familiarity of your existence. But none of the familiar will remain when we have accomplished what we set out to do. Everything will change. And your role will be fulfilled, for a time. You will go and see the world, and then return when you have done so."

"I see."

"I hope you do."

"And you do not need me to defend you."

"Indeed, I do not. Thank you for your understanding."

Once they were at the end of their meal, and they were both drinking strong coffee, Agnes having moved into stony silence, he decided it was time.

He fished into the pocket of his suit jacket, and took out a small black velvet box.

He had not seen the gem inside, but like the

house, had sent someone after it, trusting that the people he hired would fulfill his requests to his standards. Could they not do that, he would not have them in his employ.

And with a curve of his mouth, he dropped down to his knee before Agnes, the ring held out before him, and he opened the box. The gem was an emerald. And he found himself pleased about that, for a diamond was far too insipid to be on Agnes's finger.

It would look wrong. And anyone who saw her wearing it would know that.

"Oh," she said.

"Agnes," he said. "Will you marry me?"

"Yes," she said, her mouth straight, her bearing stiff and regal. And then she extended her hand, and he slipped the gem on her finger. And with one fluid, decisive moment, he pulled her off her chair, down onto his knee, and pressed his mouth to hers.

CHAPTER FOUR

AGNES HAD NEVER been kissed before. Not really.

Once, when she was fifteen, a terrible man who had been doing business with her father had grabbed her and forced his mouth onto hers.

But it had not been a kiss. It had just been violence.

She had forced her knee into that part of him that intended vile things for her and run away. This was something else. Something else entirely. His lips were hot and firm, and he smelled delicious.

Like the forest.

Like smoke and wood and spice.

He was a comfort, as he had always been. Big and strong and singular.

He wanted to send her away, and it made her feel like she was breaking apart. But right now, confusingly, after that edict, she was in his arms. And she knew that it was all part of the show. The one that dictated he put an emerald on her finger, but it was miraculous all the same. Her heart was pounding, and that pulse between her thighs over-rode any anger that resided in her veins.

Oh, how she wanted *him*. How she wanted this.

What shocked her most was his tongue. The briefest touch against her own, which set off and ignited flame in her belly that burned hot and fast and made her tremble with need.

Need for… For more of him. His hands, his…

She pulled away from him, breathing heavily.

"I have agreed," she whispered. "I think that is enough."

They left the restaurant then, and she had not seen him pay, but then, Lazarus seemed to wave his hand and things magically occurred. He did not participate in the world the way that others did. He did not do things the way common folk did.

And with each step they took back to the apart-ment, anger goaded her.

She began to tremble. For he had criticized her sword and said that he didn't need her, then told her that she could go on her way, all after she had been scrubbed and plucked in cotton, fashioned into this creature that he wished to put on display. That creature that was layered over the top of the war-rior that he had sculpted from muscle and struggle.

How was she meant to find a place in the world? Apart from him? She was all that he had made her to be, and now he was making proclamations about how he did not need her. Not really.

And she was… She was enraged.

By the time they got back to the penthouse it had only grown. When they got inside, and the elevator doors closed behind them, she shifted herself next to him, her hand on the hilt of her sword. And she was determined that she would prove her point. The doors opened again, and they went inside the penthouse.

And she did not hesitate. Instead, she exploded. She drew her sword, rounding on him, curving her leg around the back of his and taking him down to the floor as she drew her blade.

But he had barely hit the ground when she found herself being pulled forward.

He disarmed her, flinging the weapon across the room. She howled in rage as he maneuvered himself onto the top of her, his large, muscular body a weapon in and of itself as he pinned her shoulders to the ground, his eyes blazing with black fire.

"What game are you playing?" he growled.

"You doubt me," she said, breathing hard, not from exertion, for she had not begun to exert herself, but from rage and adrenaline. "You think that you can best me. You think you don't need me."

"I taught you everything you know, little one. And you are but a very small thing."

She slipped from his hold, making herself boneless before tightening her muscles yet again and climbing up onto his shoulders, curving her arm around his neck, beneath his chin and holding him fast. "*Small* does not mean *inconsequential*, my Lord."

"You test me," he growled.

"I would've broken your neck were this real."

She found herself being flipped over the top of him, lying down on her back, gazing up at him upside down, as he brought his face close to hers.

"Darling, I would've broken yours the moment you moved to draw your blade," he said, his words husky and somehow erotic.

She growled, rolling to the side and making a grab for her sword. But he was faster. He picked it up, pressing the tip of it to her chin.

"You would be no more if this were true combat," he said.

She moved away from him quickly. "I would never have stopped if this were real combat." He lunged toward her, but she moved to the side. And put her foot on the wall, climbing up above him, wrapping her legs around his neck and flinging them both to the ground with her thighs spread on either side of his shoulders. And at the same time, she reached into her jacket and took out the very small dagger that she had placed there without him realizing. She put it to his throat and grinned.

"You don't need me?" she asked. "I could destroy

you." He tried to move, and she allowed the blade to prick his skin. "You do not have the measure of me."

Then his large hands moved, but they did not harm her, instead, they went to cup her rear, squeezing her gently, and he rolled beneath her, a growl rumbling in his chest that resonated in her thighs. And she faltered. In that moment, he grabbed her hand, twisted it and relieved her of her dagger, but he did not change their positions.

"Do not play games with predators who have teeth sharper than you could ever imagine, Agnes," he said. "You are an innocent."

"I don't… I've not been innocent," she said, wiggling, trying to get away from him.

"Are you speaking of the things that you have seen in the world? Perhaps not. But you are untouched by men, are you not?"

She lifted her head high. "I'm a warrior. I opt for celibacy as a way to maintain my integrity."

"I do not," he said. "In fact I find that very few things bring the appropriate release after the heat of battle." His face was stone, his eyes dark. "Here again perhaps I have been remiss in your education."

His words sent a cascade of something unfamiliar through her body.

And suddenly, he pulled her forward. And she felt… Exposed, for all that she was wearing a skirt. But then he pushed it up over her thighs, and she knew full well that he was looking at the black lace of her panties, which would barely cover her most feminine secrets. Feminine secrets that were not secrets to him, of course, for as he said, he did not engage in celibacy.

A tangle of unnatural feelings rolled through her. And then he turned his head and he bit her thigh.

She squeaked, squirmed, as arousal warred with the slight, sharp sting of pain that his teeth left behind. And then, his one arm acting like a vise grip across her thighs, he used the other to sweep her underwear aside and expose her.

And when his mouth made contact with that molten center of her body, she squeezed her legs, using all of her strength to try to close her thighs, but he was stronger. And he only used the momentum to pull her forward, more firmly against his mouth. And he lapped at her, ate at her core while she shivered and shook. While anger turned into something much hotter. Much more forbidden.

She had wanted him. She had wanted him in ways that she didn't even have names for. But she had been certain he did not return the feeling at all. Particularly tonight when he'd said he had no need of her.

She had need of him. She always had. She had made vows in her heart to this man, and she had meant always to simply be his protector. But now this...

And then she could not deny the arousal pouring through her, not anymore. Her release was like a thunderclap.

She was accustomed to this being a quick, shameful feeling. And sometimes in the dark of her room, she did touch herself, and always, she thought of Lazarus and tried not to. Of his strength. His rough hands. Her desire to have him use them on her in a way other than sparring as they had done just now.

But this went on and on. This was something more than fantasy. This was dangerous.

This was…

She cried out and moved away from him, and he let her go.

"I…"

"Consider that a lesson," he said, looking at her with eyes more feral and beast-like than anything she'd ever seen before. "You do not have the control here. You are not more powerful than I. And if you do not learn to understand life, as I said, every facet, you will never be able to win."

He was more monster than man here, that darkness she knew lived in him on full display.

But she was more wildcat than woman just now. And she would not be bested.

And it was anger that fueled her then. Anger and a deep pride. She moved forward, pressing her hand against the front of his pants. Where she could feel that he was hard with desire.

"It seems to me as if you do not have all the power here either."

He growled and all but threw her to the side.

"We leave tomorrow for Liri."

"Is that all you have to say?" She was fractured. Broken and undone on the floor of this Parisian apartment. Disarmed and dishonored. In the moment that she had proven to him that she was not the loser, he was withdrawing.

She desired him, yes, she always had. There was no question. But this was nothing more than a bid for control to him, and she had been shattered. She would not bear it.

"There is nothing left to say," he threw out. "My point has been proven."

Anger and hurt pride spurred her on. "That you have the self-control of a rutting beast?"

"That you do not have quite the upper hand that you seem to think. You are good with a sword. But you do not know men. You do not know your own body."

"I do know my own body," she spat. "You do not get to tell me what I know. Or who I am. These are mechanical things. Any woman would have succumbed. It means nothing."

Except she was trembling inside. And it meant everything. Absolutely everything. And now she had to go and play the part of his fiancée. She still wore his ring.

In defiance, she took it off, then leaned down and dropped it into his hand.

"I do not need this now. It's only needed in public."

"You will wear it when I say."

"You are releasing me after this," she said, her pride breaking. It was one thing for him to best her in a fight. It was one thing for him to command her to be his fiancée. It was one thing for him to send her away. But to take her and manipulate her with that deep, secret attraction that she felt for him... She could not forgive it.

Because above all else she had trusted him to never use her intentionally. To never harm her or treat her callously knowingly.

And she would accept being sent away if he was going to play games with her body. For it meant nothing to him. Yes, he might have gotten hard, and she knew what that meant. Of course she did. She wasn't a child. But it was no more for her than any of this was. She was simply convenient. He would likely use her to warm his bed, in the absence of any of the usual sorts of women that he favored, and not think anything of it.

But she would.

She cared too much. And that was the problem. She cared too much, and when this was all over...

Well, she could now see the kindness of his setting her free. They had been linked together for too long.

"I believe when this is through," she reiterated. "And you have already broken the bond. The only reason that I'm doing anything that you ask me now is because I want to. I will help you with this, as repayment for all that you've done for me. But my life does not belong to you. Not now."

"Agnes…"

"No," she said. "I'm not a child. Nor am I a chess piece for you to move around at will. I swore my life to you because it was my honor to do so. I changed everything that I was because when you saved me you gave me a chance at something new. I never did it because I was being manipulated. I never did it because I was forced. I will not be toyed with now. I offer this to you as my final act of service. And then I will go. Off to make my life, as you have suggested."

"So be it. No more swords when I bid you not carry them."

"If it pleases the King."

And with a defiance that she didn't quite feel, she looked down at the front of his pants again. "For I will not engage in what else might please the King."

Then she turned on her heel and walked from the room, waiting until she was back in the bedroom before her legs collapsed beneath her.

Had it only been a day?

He had whisked her to Paris, given her a make-
over, forced her to wear skimpy clothing, engaged
her in a sword fight, gotten engaged to her and
given her the first orgasm she'd ever received from
a man.

She could scarcely cope with it all.

And then Agnes did something she had not done
since she was a girl. Because it was a weakness, and
people use your weaknesses against you. Because
there was no point to it. Because she knew better.

It didn't matter. Still, big fat tears slid down her
cheeks. Still, she dissolved into misery.

She got into bed and pulled the covers up over
her head. And she wept like she couldn't remember weeping.

She wept like her soul might fracture. Perhaps
it already had.

For the first time in eight years she had no idea
what would become of her. And she felt very much
like that sixteen-year-old in an alley, following after
a warrior and hoping that she might find a safe
place.

Your safe place is gone.

Shattered like she had been only moments earlier. Shattered along with any illusions about her
singularity.

She knew Lazarus to be a man with a healthy
sexual appetite. He took lovers. She had seen him
do it. And it had taken strips off of her heart to

watch it, but she had comforted herself with the fact that she was special. She might not be his lover, but she was his. He could not manage without her. She was his protector. And he was hers.

They occupied a singular position in each other's lives, and she had told herself it made her matter. But with a flick of his tongue over the most sensitized part of her body, he had turned her into another of his women. He would've taken her and never thought of it again.

And so, Agnes of the Dark Wood had become common, and in that way, nothing. Nothing to him, at least.

And of all the things, that hurt the worst.

CHAPTER FIVE

LAZARUS HADN'T SLEPT. He had spent the entire night going over strategies in his head.

And he cursed Agnes mentally, repeatedly, for her behavior, which had necessitated he teach her a lesson. She was barely more than a girl. She didn't know anything of the world, which was why he needed to give her some time there, why he needed to let her be harder, savvier.

And still, she would not ever be allowed to defeat him.

That lesson had been unavoidable.

She'd overestimated herself.

But it was the lingering desire he felt for her that was what he cursed most of all.

She had been so epically responsive to his touch and he had taken things much further than he'd intended.

In his effort to exert control, he'd shown he had none.

And in the end she had looked so upset that he'd wanted to take her in his arms and hold her...

No. She was not for him. But there was something about the way she fought. Furious and feral and ferocious, and she was a worthy opponent. He did not train her to be indulgent—he never had. That could have easily spelled disaster for her. He had trained her to draw blood, and he had trained her to be lethal.

What he had not expected was for her abilities to appeal to him in this way.

She was strong. Strong enough to withstand the beast inside of him. The beast that he never let out.

He liked the soft, round women that he made bed partners of back home, but they were delicate. He treated them with softness. With deference, as one should.

But the lean muscle of Agnes's body demanded to be tested.

Tested her he had, but he had not imagined he might find himself tested as well. That strong body begging him to give it his worst—pleasure and pain alike.

But it would not be borne, not again.

And he was impatient. The meeting between himself and Alexius was sure to be... Tense. He would have to evaluate just what Alexius was thinking, what he wanted.

He would be staying in the palace. That place

that was little more than an echo in his memory. And Agnes was nowhere to be seen.

"Agnes," he roared.

And she did not appear. He stormed across the room, as if her bad mood was her fault, and he flung open the doors to her bedroom.

She sat up, and he saw the rosy crests of her breasts. She was not wearing any clothes.

And his control suffered another mighty blow. It would not be endured.

She gasped and covered herself. "What are you doing?"

"You overslept," he growled.

"I have not overslept," she said. "You didn't tell me when to wake up."

"You never sleep past one."

"I am never in Paris."

Another truth sizzled between them.

"Indeed not."

"I have no patience for you today," she said.

Agnes did not usually snipe at him.

Nor did she usually wear his ring.

Or shatter beneath his mouth.

Or display her breasts.

"What happened to *my Lord*? What happened to *Your Highness*?"

"What happened to sanity?"

He stormed out of her room, and she appeared a moment later, looking freshly scrubbed and angry, back in the clothing that she had arrived in yesterday.

"We depart for Liri in an hour."

"It is a private plane, so you and I both know that you just decided that right this moment, and you had no preexisting plan, and you are now making it my problem that you didn't tell me."

"Quiet yourself," he said.

"I would rather contend with a toothless bulldog than you right at the moment."

He smiled and made sure to show all of his teeth. "Not toothless. And you cannot wear that."

"Why not?"

"We will get off the plane and have an immediate audience with my brother."

"You have arranged this?"

"It will be so."

"You cannot just make demands of him. He doesn't care that you're the King of the kingdom he does not recognize."

"Perhaps not. But we will show that I am not to be trifled with. Eventually, that is what he will learn."

"What do you intend to do to him?"

"All we're doing is fact-finding at the moment. We need his trust. We need to learn everything we can about Liri. About the kingdom as it is structured. About the weaknesses in the palace. About those who may not be loyal to him."

"I know how to run a con, Lazarus," she said, using his first name aloud, which she never did. "I only never imagined running one with you."

"This is not a con, Agnes. This is not about lining my pockets with money. It is not about benefiting myself. It is returning to my people what is rightfully theirs."

"Have you forgotten that you're Lirian. You might have grown up in the wood, but you are not one of them."

The words were like that dagger she carried sheathed at her beautiful thigh. He had not forgotten, of course he hadn't. That it was the blood of the disloyal—those who had sacrificed their child to a forest. The blood of the murderous traitor—the ancestor who had crushed a people beneath his fist in the name of power. That was the blood that ran through his veins.

He could never hope to have as much honor as the people he'd adopted.

"And neither are you," he said.

A dangerous thing thrashed about in his chest.

"I'm aware. But I'm not the one who is intent on deposing their own brother."

"Perhaps not," he said. "But you know how it is. My life belongs to Agamemnon. My life belongs to the people. I survived that I might complete this task. Whatever else happens doesn't matter."

"Nothing?"

He shook his head, the blank, dark black hole in his soul feeling particularly cavernous at the moment. "No. Nothing. There is nothing else for me but this vengeance. But it is more than vengeance— it is a restoration of justice."

"What am I to wear?"

Unbidden, his mind went back to the sight of her breasts. They were beautiful. Just as she was. All that well-honed muscle. He would've said that was not his particular type for a bed partner. But there was a roughness that he fantasized about…

She was suited to that. She would hold up against the pounding that he wished to unleash…

Never.

Agnes was his the way another person might own a rare artifact. It was the way of their tradition. She was to be valued, cared for and honored. He was her master, but if she fell into disrepair, he and he alone would bear the shame of it.

"Yes," he said. "The red dress."

As if the devil was in him, suggesting that.

"Isn't that a bit much for meeting with your brother."

"I should like you to wear the red dress. With red lipstick. Go. See that it is done."

She vanished and returned very quickly, her hair down, nothing but the barest hint of mascara on her lashes, along with the bright red lipstick he had commanded. She was stunning like that. It was only truly beautiful women who could play such games with makeup and win. "Have I met with your approval, my Lord?"

"You please me," he said.

He approached her, and he heard her breath catch in her throat, saw her pulse quicken in her neck. "Now you must only put on a convincing performance as a woman who is madly in love with me."

"I would like to eviscerate you with my teeth presently, so it will be a challenge."

And in spite of himself, he felt a kick of lust hit hard right in his stomach. He would like very much to have her use her teeth on him. And he would use his own on her in return.

He didn't know where these thoughts were coming from. These aberrations. He was not a man who was controlled by his appetites. They were an appetite like any other, and when he felt the need, he indulged them. But that was it. Right now, his desire for her was intruding. In ways he did not appreciate or accept.

"Come," he said.

"What about all of my things?"

"They will be gathered and brought. No need to fret."

"I am not fretting."

Almost as soon as they were down in the lobby, a pair of men dressed all in black went back up to the penthouse.

"They will bring all of your things to the plane."

"Well, why bother to leave without our things?"

"I thought you might like a pastry. Perhaps some coffee."

"In a gown? At ten in the morning?"

"We are in France, and we are newly engaged. We may do whatever we like."

And it was difficult for her to be angry once she was settled with a strong coffee and a pastry, and he could see that it enraged her on a new level. That she could not deny his hospitality.

She never could deny food.

She nibbled at the pastry in a rather delicate manner, which he found amusing, as he knew she was not delicate at all.

"Satisfied?"

"Not by half," she said, stiffly.

"Now you're just being spiteful."

"Perhaps I'm enjoying being spiteful. I've had to be nothing but eminently grateful to you for the past eight years, and do you know, it gets very tiring."

"Yes. I imagine it so much more tiring than the life that you led before."

"You don't know anything about the life I led before."

"I certainly do. Your father was a con man."

"Yes. Who tangled with the wrong men in France nearly a decade ago. But what else do you know? Where else that I lived? Where I'm from?"

He took a sip of his coffee and stared at her. "Clearly you're American."

"Am I?"

"Yes. Originally. Though you do speak a great many languages."

"With great proficiency," she snapped. "But yes, I was born in America."

"And where?"

"Ohio."

He laughed. "Where is Ohio?"

"1997." She answered it with a straight face, and he did not understand what she meant by that. "It's in the Midwest," she said.

"Yes. Flyover states, I hear."

"A lot of snobbery for a man who was raised in a forest by people who are little better than wolves."

"They are a lot better than the wolves, darling," he said, yet again making certain to flash his teeth, hoping she took note of his scars. "The wolves would've simply eaten me. And were I a wolf, I would've simply eaten you." But the truth that he in fact had eaten her settled between them heavily.

And desire roared in his gut.

"My mother died when I was four," she said. "I don't think we were normal even then. I think my mother helped my father with his scams. But I don't know for sure. I... My first memory of my father is him telling me to pretend to be lost and crying. He taught me how to pick pockets. He taught me to take advantage of little old ladies. And they never sus-pected. Because I was small and cute. He taught me to use every asset that I had. To hurt other people."

Oh, Agnes. He might have been savaged by wolves.

She had been raised by them.

And he wondered if he had not given her enough credit for that. If he had not given enough space to her wounds.

"A sad life."

"The only life I knew. Until this one."

It reinforced the fact that he had to send her off on her own.

"You will enjoy a life on your own terms, I think."

"I don't know that I will. But I suppose I have to try."

When the car stopped, he leaned in and pressed his thumb to her lips, then rubbed her lipstick gently. Most of it coming off on his thumb.

"What are you doing?"

"I would like my brother to have to imagine where on my body that lipstick ended up."

"What does it matter?" she said, her cheeks turn-ing pink.

"It matters a great deal. If I'm to present myself as a man in love, it must be believable. He must believe that this is real. That I am changed. Soft."

"He never knew you were hard to begin with."

He had hurt Agnes last night. Not her body, her heart, and he'd seen it. She had already lived with those who had been callous with her.

And it made him want to give her this. So she was not alone in her sharing.

"Do you know what I remember of my life?"

"What?"

"Him. I remember my brother. And how I looked up to him. We played out on the palace lawn all the time. But the forest always fascinated me. I couldn't turn away from it. Even though I knew it was supposed to be dangerous. Part of me didn't believe it. I had to wonder why the stories were in place the way that they were. It was as if it was to... Deter people for some reason. And yes, I know. Wolves."

"Your youngest brother..."

He shrugged. "I never knew him. I don't mean to be cruel, but I don't grieve him."

"Of course not," she said. But she didn't sound convinced.

"I understand now. Why they didn't want us to go in there. They didn't want us to know. They didn't want anyone in Liri to know. Those people were almost snuffed out. By a power-mad King who wanted all of the land. By a man who didn't respect the old ways. The old traditions. That man was my great-grandfather. And it is up to me to make right what was done wrong. Because no one else will. These people are owed their land. They are owed freedom."

He waited to feel something in connection with that. But he did not.

Instead, he could simply feel the burn of her mouth against his thumb. Feel the red against his skin like a flame.

"And you wish to do that. You feel that strongly about it."

He felt nothing. But that was a sad state of affairs for most of his life.

It was as if he had left emotion behind along with his title. As if he had left it behind along with his mother and father.

They had left him behind quickly enough. They had been quick to announce his death. He had been informed by Agamemnon when it had happened, and he'd looked it up for himself his first time in Paris. He was not necessary. He was the spare, after all, and there was a reason that those in line for leadership in land ownership were referred to in such a fashion. He had done research on his own disappearance when he had gone off into the world. They had not, it seemed, mourned for long, and why would they. One child could be replaced easily with the next. And so they had done.

It was fate. He had accepted it. He was not mortally wounded by it. In a sense, it was how it must be.

For he had a goal to accomplish, a purpose higher than himself. And it was what mattered.

Not feelings. Those unreliable, unwieldy things that could be counted on for nothing. "It is what I must do," he repeated.

When the plane landed in Liri, he took her arm. "No sword?"

She looked down at the gown, which fitted to her form perfectly. "Where would I put one?"

"You and I both know that you are resourceful."

They began to disembark from the plane, moving slowly down the steps. He was aware that there were photographers. He paid them no mind.

"There is one," she said, tilting her face up toward him. And if he didn't know any better, he would say that she was madly in love with him. For her face was radiant, her smile wide, and her lipstick smudged just so, as he had designed it. "Strapped just to my inner thigh. If you were to put your hand up my gown and feel me there, you would find it. But you might get more than you bargained for."

He ground his teeth as her words had what he could only imagine was the desired effect on him. He studied her profile, her flat, curved nose and upturned upper lip, which gave her a regal bearing, her dark, unknowable eyes. She was a con woman, as she had reminded him only yesterday. Raised to lie, to fit in wherever she had to, to accomplish whatever she must by whatever means necessary. And what an actress. It was impossible to say what she wished him to glean from her words. Perhaps it was a threat. Perhaps she intended to take control as she had tried to do last night, by ensuring that he was aroused.

Sadly for her he did not exist in shame or regret. He only lived for the next moment.

"Let us both hope you've no need of it."

"But if there is need, I will use it. Remember, I am free now." She looked at him, her eyes liquid.

"As you wish, Agnes. For if one tightens their hand with too much force around a fragile thing, it shall shatter, and then what good does it do anyone? Except ensuring that no one else can have it."

"I'm not fragile," she whispered.

"I think you are more fragile than you believe."

"You're wrong."

"You shattered beneath my mouth easily enough."

Heat smoldered between them, burned in his veins. The memory pulsed between them and made a liar of him. For he was not living in the present moment, but in the moment when he'd touched her not like a teacher, but like a lover.

"I cannot wait to be free of you."

But she only smiled for all to see, and only he knew that she was venomous with him.

They got into a car, which drove them along the winding road that led to the palace. That led close to their home. The edge of the Dark Wood. They did not come and go from the country through this way. Rather they left out the other side of the forest, and used airports of the neighboring nation, typically.

A habit. For Lazarus had been in hiding from Liri for a very long time, and moreover, there was such an animosity between his people and the Lirians… An animosity the Lirians did not even know existed.

At least, as far as he could remember. He had been such a small boy when he had wandered away from home. Then he had not known that it would be the last time he would see the palace. That it would be the last time he would see his brother.

His mother and father…

The castle.

The memories that washed over him were strange and stretched. Not something that a person could make sense of. Not easily. For they were lost somewhere in the mists of childhood, twisted by that lens, and once again warped by the reality that was now before him. The way that he saw the place as a man well into his thirties.

More than thirty years he'd been away from home.

No. It was not home. The wood was home. Those were his people.

By blood, he might be a Lirian, and for that he would have to atone. But in his soul, he knew who he was. These soft things were not his. These people were not his.

This palace was not his home.

Just as this land was not theirs.

"Are you well?" she asked.

She asked the question stiffly, and he could tell that she resented feeling anything about his mental state at all.

"I am as I ever am," he responded.

"A nonanswer," she said, her words clipped. "As ever."

"We are not friends, Agnes."

He could feel that land much harder than he'd intended. Or perhaps not. Perhaps he'd wanted to distance her.

"I am aware of that, my Lord."

But there was no difference in her tone, and there was no affection either. He had broken something last night. But he was not the sort of man who had the capacity to regret it.

The car pulled up to the front of the palace, and they got out.

"Announce us," he said to the man who had driven them. He wasted no time in obeying Lazarus's command. And then the palace doors were open to them, wide, and the procession of staff came out, standing sentry along the lines of the high-gloss corridors.

There was no army, no suspicion.

The staff allowed him in simply because he had a genetic link to Alexius. Who believed that they were brothers, in spite of the years that stood between them.

His own fault.

He had advised him.

Played the part of… Well, he had played the part of brother when Alexius and his Tinley had separated, and had told him to reconcile with her.

Lazarus still felt what he'd told him then was true. He'd found a woman who loved him—something Lazarus himself never thought to have—and he should keep her.

But it remained to be seen if they would have a long life together.

Something was uncomfortable, pinching at his chest, and if he had been another man, he might've called it guilt. But he was not another man. And he could not be.

He moved himself closer to Agnes, holding her arm in his, and Agnes, to her credit, remained serene. That warrior's posture became something softer, more elegant. And yet, he could see in every line of her being that she was a fighter. He could only hope that his brother did not perceive the same thing he did.

A man dressed all in black came to stand alongside them. "Allow me to announce you to His Highness," he said.

"Please do," Lazarus responded.

"And how shall I announce you?"

"King Lazarus of the Wood," he responded. "And Agnes."

The man went ahead of them, and Agnes's shoulders wiggled. "And Agnes," she repeated, in a poor imitation of his voice and accent, in his opinion.

"I'm sorry, do you have an issue?"

"I've no title," she responded. "I am Agnes, warrior of the wood, sworn protector of the King."

"You are not," he said. "Not here. And anyway, I was given the impression that you had abdicated your position."

"Yes. Though I will still be fulfilling it here."

"Agnes, my fiancée, and nothing more."

She looked flattened by that, and he tried not to care.

A moment later, the two of them were ushered into the throne room. Alexius did not sit on a throne, and neither did Tinley, his fiancée. Rather, they were sitting in what looked to be a regular, casual receiving area, plush and welcoming. There were trays of sweets, and he stole a glance at Agnes, who was looking pleased by this development.

"Brother," Alexius said, standing. His older brother was nearly his height, possessing more of a lean strength than Lazarus's own. Tinley was petite, with massive amounts of red hair. She was soft. She had a cat sitting on her lap.

Agnes saw the creature, a line pleating between her brows, as her mouth turned down into a frown. It was exceedingly Agnes to be confused by the cat.

"I'm glad that you came," Alexius said. "We have so much to discuss."

"Thank you for the invitation," Lazarus said. "I'm newly engaged, and it is good for Agnes and I to spend time here. Good that she gets to know you as well."

"I saw that," Alexius said. "Very newly engaged. As it was in the news this morning."

"A resurrection and an engagement. A big month for me."

Alexius chuckled. "Indeed. Come, brother, we have much to discuss. We can leave Tinley and Agnes to get to know one another."

CHAPTER SIX

AGNES HAD A feeling that was her cue to sit, but she found she did not want to. She was fractured still from last night, and the plane ride with Lazarus had done nothing to make it better. The way that he had touched her mouth... And the way that he insisted on continuing to bring up her... Shattering. And now she was here, talking to this woman they were intent on betraying. This woman who had a... A cat.

That she kept as a pet.

"You can sit," Tinley said, smiling brightly.

"Thank you," Agnes said.

She took a seat as far away from the cat as possible.

"Are you allergic to cats?" Tinley asked. "Because I can send him out."

"Oh, there's no need. It's only that... It is strange to me. That there should be an animal indoors."

And cats frightened her. They were disconcerting. And this one, called Algie, had large yellow eyes that made her feel seen.

But she would not say that.

"Oh, yes. Alexius finds it strange also, but I do not give him a choice."

She wrinkled her nose. "You tell him what to do?"

Tinley smiled happily. "Yes. Occasionally. I have many animals inside the palace. He does not like it. They had their own room. They were not allowed in ours. Though, there are often exceptions made. When I wish them to be made."

"Lazarus is not quite so malleable."

"I wouldn't call Alex malleable," Tinley said. "Only that he is more so now than he was when I first came to live at the palace. By which I mean when I was a child."

"You are much younger than him," Agnes said.

"Yes. I was engaged to his brother. His… His younger brother… Younger than Lazarus."

"Yes," Agnes said. "I know of him. The one who was killed."

"Yes," Tinley said.

She looked sad, though it was not heartbroken sort of grief.

"Are you in love with Alex?" Agnes asked.

She wondered, because Lazarus had been moved by their connection. She wondered, because Alexius shared blood with Lazarus.

And in spite of herself, Agnes loved him.

"Yes," Tinley said. "It became clear to me later that I always was. Always. It was only that… I did have a great deal of affection for his brother. I still feel badly about what happened. Very sad. But I recognize now that I did not love him like that, and never would have. We would not have… We would not have worked."

"You can be certain about that?"

"A certain as I can be about anything. Alex was the one I was always meant for. I don't think Dionysus had to die in order for that to be so. I fear rather we would've collapsed a monarchy with our need to be together eventually. But fortunately, that did not have to be. I mean… Unfortunately… You know."

"Yes," she said. She thought of the many fortunate unfortunate things that had to occur in order for her to be in Lazarus's life.

Though, she was not certain now how fortunate she was. No. She only felt mean toward him at the moment.

And this woman… In spite of her cat… She was very nice, and she found that disconcerting. All things considered.

"How long will you be staying with us? Of course you are welcome to stay as long as you like. There are other houses on the grounds. You could stay in the palace, or you could stay at some of the estates."

"Whatever it is Lazarus wishes."

Tinley tilted her head to the side. "How do you know my brother-in-law?"

Agnes figured that in situations such as this the answer that was closest to the truth was likely the best.

"He saved my life," she said. "And I... I have loved him ever since."

The words sat in the room and seemed to fill the space. She had never admitted this out loud before. She had no one to admit it to.

But they were true.

And they resonated in her soul as they did from the walls around her.

She loved him, and she felt no shame in it. Not here. It was part of her, as was her loyalty to him.

"You are younger than he is," she said, turning that question that Agnes had asked back around on her.

"Yes," Agnes confirmed. "I am. But he has long been my protector, and he is... He is a man of honor."

"And you love him," Tinley said.

"More than anything in the world."

And the thing she hated most of all was that it seemed very close to the truth of the matter.

Even as she was angry. Even if she was sitting here next to a cat.

It was soon that Alexius and Lazarus returned.

"You may stay as long as you like," Alex said. "I have offered Lazarus the east wing of the palace. It is both of yours, if you wish."

"My thanks," Lazarus said. "I look forward to our getting to know one another. To this restoration."

And Agnes knew that there was truth beneath those words. But the restoration that Lazarus had a vision of was hardly what Alexius would be expecting.

"I would join you for dinner tonight, but I have an engagement in England I cannot escape. Instead, I will have something special laid out for you and your fiancée."

Agnes's stomach tightened. How many more special dinners could she possibly endure with Lazarus? Particularly if they ended in sword fights. Which ended in…

"Much appreciated."

Lazarus paused. "Make sure that the spread is heavy on sweets. My fiancée has a fondness for cake."

He took her arm and led her from the sitting room, moving toward what she assumed was the east wing. She had never seen any place this grand. It was a palace that seemed to be built from foundational stones of the earth. Old and filled with history, layered over the top with precious gems. It was true there were riches in the forest, but it was different than this.

"Here it is," he said. "My inheritance, as it were."

"It is a beautiful palace."

"Exactly as I remember it," he said, his voice taking a dark turn. "Shining and glittering. I thought that perhaps it was a trick of my imagination. For no place could... No place could be quite this grand."

"Is that so?"

"It is so," he said. "And yet... It is also real. This place. I was happy here."

She stopped walking. She had never heard him speak of his family in that way. He didn't speak of them at all. He spoke of it in matter-of-fact terms. How he had once been a prince of Liri, but then had gone into the wood.

But he did not speak of it with softness. And even now, she wouldn't call it... She wouldn't exactly call it softness. It was something more. But there was emotion to this, and that was something he did not typically demonstrate. The corridors were long, and suddenly the glitter seemed to take on a sinister aspect.

"Yes," he said. "My rooms were here."

That statement hit her full in the chest. It wasn't the place that was darker, it was his mood.

Deeply so.

And of course. For this had been the place that

he… That he'd started his life, the place that he had lost forever after he had wandered away.

And suddenly, she felt a deep kinship to him, and she had never experienced that before at all. And she didn't know why she should. Because she hadn't started life in a palace, but it was simply… Perhaps it was simply knowing that there was something you should have that you did not. A loyalty from your parents that you should have that didn't exist. A sense of home that you were denied.

They might be from very different backgrounds; they might be from very different places, but that was the same.

It was the same.

The bedchambers that had been appointed to them were definitely not children's rooms, and the splendor of them stole her breath, took her focus away from the sadness that had lodged itself in her chest at least.

It was so opulent. But the large bed at the center of the space was what made her heart freeze.

"Do not worry," he said, his voice dripping with humor. Very dark humor. "I am accustomed to sleeping on rocks, Agnes. The bed is yours."

"I am also strong enough to withstand a few nights on the floor."

"Excellent. Perhaps we might both curl up on the floor as animals, both to prove the point to one another, and the bed can sit there unused, soft and utterly wasted."

"I shall do what I please, in the end. I shall do as pleases myself from here on out."

"Yes. The emancipation of Agnes has been quite proclaimed."

"It is as you commanded."

"I did not command you to leave entirely. Of course, I will not stop you from doing so, but I am very aware that you dishonor the pact which we have made."

"I dishonor nothing," she said.

"So be it. You will also continue to fulfill this role as I see fit. My brother has said that we are allowed use of this entire facility. Indeed, he has suggested that you and I make use of the baths prior to our dinner. Apparently, it is to be an exquisite affair. One set up on the terrace, well lit and brilliant. A reminder, I'm certain, of all the opulence that I missed growing up."

"He likes you. Don't you feel any guilt about that?"

She might feel some pity for Lazarus, but it was just impossible. To be here and be around Alexius and Tinley and not feel a certain measure of guilt. How was this not a con? Tricking people. Fooling them. Gaining their trust and breaking it.

She had done it countless times as a child with her father.

Stealing people's money. But worse, stealing their trust. Stealing their hope.

Creating a world where people would not be as generous, because she had been part of taking advantage of it.

She had made the world a worse place in the first sixteen years of her life, and she might not have been in charge of the scenarios, but it was all the same in the end. The outcome was the same. In this...

What if he did kill Alexius?

What if he broke all these people who simply had the misfortune of descending from a people that had committed gross acts. What if there was another way?

And they weren't looking for it because the easiest way was the path of the sword?

The easiest way was the path of lies?

And here they were, taking advantage of this hospitality and pretending to mean things to each other that they did not.

"What?"

"He trusts you," she said. "He trusts you, and he wishes to be a brother to you. I do not approve of this."

She loved her home in the wood. She loved the people there. She felt loyalty to him, but first her loyalty was to Lazarus, and his very soul.

And to honor.

She could not find the honor here.

"This is our moment," he said. "Our chance to take hold of that which has been denied us all this time. Is it not worthy, Agnes? Are you too good? Perhaps that is because it is not truly your right."

"That isn't it. It's not what I think. I just think… You are not your great-grandfather, any more than Alexius is. Maybe there's a way to restore what our people are owed without bloodshed. Maybe there's a way where you can still be brothers."

"I do not believe that such a thing is possible."

"Only because you were not given a path to that way. But perhaps you have to make your own."

"What makes you an expert? You, Agnes, who have no family name, because you have no family."

She gritted her teeth. "I am an expert because anytime I am emulating a behavior that my father would have engaged in, then I can be most certain that it is wrong. My father was always a coward. He always took the route of least resistance. The least amount of work. He wanted nothing more than his own comfort, and he cared nothing for the needs of others. Do you know why? Because it is hard. It is hard to try to get what you deserve, and be concerned with your own morality. And my father never did anything that was hard. Ever. Perhaps I believe that you are strong enough to do hard things. The more I find myself feeling as if I am engaging in another low-level con as my father would've done, the more I am certain that this cannot be the answer."

The look he gave her was filled with iron. And she had the sense that had she been anyone but Agnes he would not have allowed her to speak in such a fashion. In fact he would not allow her to speak at all.

"You speak of things you don't understand," he said. "You live because I rescued you. You exist because of the help that I have given. Help that your father did not give you. You dare compare me to him? You dare compare me to him when you know full well that he died and left you alone, while I thought nothing of risking myself to elevate you. What I do is not for my own personal enrichment, but for honor. But for the restoration of the people. But to heal the scars of the nation. That is why I do what I do. If you cannot understand that, so be it. And if you must leave now, then leave."

Fear slammed into her chest. "I will not leave," she said.

The small note of terror in her voice seemed to call her a liar. All of the stances that she had taken since last night, her proclamations that she would strike out on her own… What did they mean? They might as well have been notes written on paper and cast into the wind for all that they mattered. For she had proven now that she feared—deeply—that future without him.

She did. Oh, how she did. And that wounded her to confess it.

"If you have no honor, then leave."

And she could not allow him that. Would not.

"I will finish what I have sworn to finish. But I will not go along quietly. I will not. They are good people. And I've spoken my piece."

"Good. Have yourself a rest, and then, we will make use of the baths."

Her skin prickled. "Why?"

"It is not yours to question me."

And with that, he left her there in the bedchamber, disappearing into another part of the wing.

And she did not know what would happen next. For the first time in a very long time, she did not know.

Lazarus was still angry about the confrontation he had with Agnes a couple of hours earlier. But he was intent on doing exactly as his brother had bade him. He was not here, so he would not see whether or not Lazarus and Agnes used the baths, but he had offered it. And it was entirely possible that news of whether or not they had would filter back to Alexius. And he must do nothing that would cause him to question Lazarus's motives.

He went into the bathroom and stripped naked, putting on one of the robes that had been provided for them. And then he took the other one that was hanging in there and brought it out to the bedchamber, where he found Agnes, sitting on the bed, looking angry. She was still wearing the red dress that she had had on since that morning.

And the idea of being alone with her in the baths made his blood hot.

"Put this on," he said.

She looked up at him. "Now?"

"Agnes," he said. "I haven't time for you to develop a sense of maidenly modesty. We are fighting a battle. Take your dress off, put the robe on."

And perhaps it was more for him than for her that he issued this challenge. Perhaps it was about proving that he was a man in control.

A man who could still keep Agnes in her proper place. As he must.

Her expression was scathing as she stood from the bed and reached around behind her back. Then she turned away from him, lowering the zipper, and it took him a moment to realize that he was standing there staring, his gaze fixed on her body. And even when he realized, he did not alter course.

Rather he clenched his jaw, tightening his hands into fists as the scarlet fabric dropped from her golden skin and slithered down onto the floor. She unhooked her bra with deft ease, and then pushed her panties down her thighs. Stepping out of them when they reached the floor. He had a good sense of the shape of Agnes's body. They had trained together, after all, engaging in intense physical hand-to-hand combat. But seeing all that ripe golden skin was different than simply having an understanding of it. Her rear was round and well muscled like the rest of her, but still looked as if it would make a pleasing handful. Too quickly, she slid the robe on, covering her body, and then she turned to face him. And he managed to will his body into absolute submission. Managed to keep himself from getting hard. He was a man of eminent control, and so it would be the same with her.

"Ready," she said, giving him an evil look.

"I'll lead the way."

One good thing about testing himself with Agnes's body and her beauty was that it gave him a chance to focus on something other than the hauntingly familiar halls of the palace. He did not wish to have memories. Not of this place. He did not wish to think of his childhood here.

That boy that had been born in this palace was dead. He had been dead to his family from the moment he had set foot in the forest, and he must be dead to Lazarus himself. It was the only way. The only real thing. And so those memories were nothing. This was nothing.

They went down to the lowest part of the palace, as Alexius had instructed, but this room was not a typical bath.

It was… An indoor river that seemed to flow

beneath the palace, lined with gems, which glittered on the walls.

He looked at Agnes, whose eyes were wide, her mouth dropped open into a perfect circle.

"You like it," he said.

"Yes," she responded.

"I do not remember this," he said.

And he detested the words as soon as they were out of his mouth, because he was not giving any credence to his memory at all. Whether it was there or not.

"I imagine this was not a place for children."

It was true. This was a place of very adult luxury, and he knew well enough to know that it existed in part for debauchery.

For no place so lavish could avoid being the site of many a sexual adventure.

He dropped his robe without preamble or warning, and Agnes's cheeks went scarlet. She looked away from him quickly, not even bothering to pretend that she was not shocked and horrified by the sight of his bare body.

And it restored a sense of power to him, which he appreciated. He stepped away from her, and toward the water, so immersing himself and covering anything she might not have seen before.

He looked back at her, but she was still not looking at him. Her hands were at the belt of her robe.

And he could see the moment she decided to meet his challenge.

And then his control was badly shaken. For her hands began to work at the knot on her robe, and in that moment, there was nothing. No vengeance. No palace. Nothing but this.

Agnes.

His strong, brave Agnes, removing her robe from her shoulders and exposing her entire body to his view. Those high, round breasts, her strong, lean body, and yet gently curved hips. And that dark thatch of curls between her legs, that place where he had tasted, and suddenly his mouth watered for more. He was hard as an iron bar beneath the surface of the water, and he was only grateful that she could not see. Because she would see this as exactly what it was. A weakness.

He was not doing well in fighting against his desire for this woman.

And how could that be so?

For they were bonded in a way that made that impossible.

And yet.

Did she not break the bond?

She had. She was leaving.

Leaving.

And suddenly, suddenly, he saw his world for what it was. Dark and devoid. But there was something about her that made it feel like it might be more. Something about her that made his life seem more… More like a life. And she would remove herself from it. Entirely. And he no longer had any say in the matter. For he could not… He could not keep her in a cage.

Could you not?

And for what purpose?

But if she was no longer his and she was no longer under his protection? Not in the way that he had always seen himself as her protector. And if that was the case, did it not just make them a man and a woman in this moment?

A man and a woman in this space.

And she was… She was glorious.

Brave and strong, a goddess as she began to step into the water.

And she did it all because she was angry with him. She did it all filled with spite. But it made no real matter to him.

For she was here.

The one and only thing that had ever truly been his.

Agnes.

She got into the water, up to her waist, covering that delectable space between her legs, but leaving her breasts bare to his view.

"Why do you look at me like that?"

"You're beautiful," he said. "And I am a man."

"I thought you were rock."

"I am rather hard at the moment."

She blinked. "I've not ever known you to make jokes. Particularly not of that nature."

"I've not ever known myself to make them either," he said, not certain as to what was happening now.

He took a step toward her.

"Don't," she said.

And he stopped.

"Don't want?"

"Do not… Do not play games with me. I'm not a plaything. You used my body against me last night. Used a feeling that I'm not familiar with to make a mockery of me, and I hate it. I would beg you not to do that. Not ever again."

He looked at her, and he felt all the need contained in the universe echo inside him. "And if I said I simply wanted you?"

She looked away. "Why?"

A good question. And suddenly the answer seemed clear.

"Because you're going to go out into the world after this, a free woman, you say. And I want… I want to be part of teaching you what it means to be a woman. Have I not always been there for you? Have I not always been your teacher?"

She looked away from him. "I hardly think…"

"Let us not think."

He was angry all of a sudden, that he should

want this, want her, here in this place, and feel denied. This palace…

How he wanted her. And he didn't want to be denied. Not anymore. Not her, not anything.

No, he did not wish to exhibit restraint. There were hard lessons that she needed to learn. The world was unforgiving, and she would have to be strong. She was strong in many ways. In the ways of battle. But she did not understand this sort of fight, and she had no tolerance for it.

She would have to learn or find herself harmed in the world.

And was that not the function of a mentor?

He had been made to face a pack of dogs after nearly being consumed by wolves.

She would face him.

Reckon with the need she had created in him.

Her eyes went wide and she backed away from him, against the wall, the gems glittering behind her, the reflection of the water casting glowing waves over her skin.

She was beautiful. And he didn't believe her showing of fear. Not for one moment. For she could attack him if she saw fit. Best him in any sort of battle that she so chose. So why play the uncertain maiden? It made no sense.

"Where has your fire gone?"

"Don't," she said. "You've already proven that my defenses against you are not where they should be. You've already proven that you could take advantage of me if you had a mind."

"What makes you think I require this display of you?"

Her eyes sharpened. "What makes you think it's for you? Am I not allowed to have my own feelings? You're right. I've never been touched by a man. Not like that. Not before yesterday. Not… I had one man, once, attempt to have his way with me. But he was rough and violent. And I fought him off. But this? You made me desire you. And you are supposed to be… You are supposed to be safe. But you've gone and changed the rules."

"I have," he said. "You attacked me with a sword, Agnes. And you act like my giving you an orgasm is somehow worse? More of a betrayal?"

"Well, yes. Surely that wasn't the first time you've ever been attacked by a sword."

"Why don't you show me what you're made of."

"Why?"

"I like your spirit."

She laughed, the sound hollow. "You don't like my spirit. You only like it when you can bend me to your will. When you can be amused at it. A waste of my spirit."

He braced his hands on the wall, on either side of her shoulders, and her breasts came very close to brushing against his chest. "What is it that scares you the most? That this is unknown? Or that you desire me."

"What does desire have to do with anything? I am a woman, after all. For all that I have attempted to fashion myself into a warrior, and only that, you have not done the same. I have watched you satisfy your urges with many women. They come and go from your chamber in an alarming pattern. No, it is only women who must become strong by denying their desire. By denying their gender. And so this… This is only the same. The same as you and all those other women. I have a desire, and you are here. You've taken your clothes off." She looked over him. "It is natural that I might think of how things could be between us. But you…"

He grabbed hold of her hands and quickly wrapped his fingers around her wrists, drawing them up over her head. Pinning her against the wall. And then he did press his chest flush with hers, feel the excited tips of her breasts against his chest. "And yet you do not desire another man, do you?"

She was breathing hard, her eyes wide, but she did not fight him, and he knew that she could. That she could make him very uncomfortable, very quickly.

"I don't know any other men."

But she would. Someday she would give all this strength and softness to someone else. It was part of allowing her into the world. A part of allowing her to experience time away from him. He had taught her to fight. He had taught her to protect herself. Why shouldn't he teach her this? Why shouldn't he be the one to teach her all that her body could do?

She was the one intent on breaking their bond for good. The one intent on shifting the power balance. And why then should he keep her at arm's length?

And why... Why should she get to dictate what happened between them? So many pronouncements from this woman he had cared for. From this woman he had...

There was no deeper bond than the one that they shared. It did not exist. Not in the whole of the universe.

And she wanted to walk away from him completely.

"What are you afraid of, little one?"

She lifted her chin. "Not you."

"Are you strong enough then, to have me this way."

She squared her shoulders, her chest pressing forward. "And what will I get for it? In the end, I will go on my way. And what will I have gotten? For becoming one of the many women who have paraded through your bedroom. One of the many women to satisfy your baser animal urges. I would be better, I think, for having turned you away. For who is strong enough to do that?"

"But you want me? So what does it matter?"

"Because I have been inconsequential. I have been nothing. And in you, in the wood, I found a home. It matters. And if you just wish to use me as you do your other women, to combat the fact that I have defied you, to make me into something that you forget... Well then, I want nothing to do with it. Nothing at all."

He looked at this woman, this woman whose life had been so linked to his own. Who was so different from every woman he had ever desired.

"You are Agnes," he said, for it was all he could say. He was never at a loss. Not ever. And yet, she put him there. "I would never confuse you with another."

And he looked at her, really looked at her, and he saw that her fear was real. But with it, she was strong. With it, she was exhibiting great strength.

And it occurred to him then, he didn't know why he had not thought of this before. But he had to keep her. He would have to keep her with him forever.

He had wanted to give her distance from him because he had not accepted the truly honorable thing to do.

To bind her to him forever. In every way.

The truth was, he could not have Agnes in halves. Once he wanted her, he had to let her go...

Or make her his bride.

For she was his in a profound sort of way that he

could not give voice to. His in a way that went beyond logic. And she would need… Not this.

Shows of strength, battle, it was what Agnes knew. And she had been used. Many times. Used by her father in order to accomplish his ends.

But had anyone ever worked to gain her trust. Really and truly. Had anyone ever done anything for her. It was clear now what she wanted. Agnes wanted to feel special. And as for himself, Lazarus knew nothing about feelings. What he knew was strength. What he knew was power. A sense of duty and honor. And a sense of ownership.

He knew care, because it was what one did when they had a responsibility to another person. Yes, he knew about those things.

But he had to figure out just how to show those things to her. To find a way to reach her so that this time when he pleasured her she was not hurt or upset.

He had to try something new.

And he took a step away from her.

"Enjoy your bath."

"What?"

"This should be for you. You have been without comfort for so long."

"Why?"

"You're right. I have no right to make demands of you. You… Agnes, you must be cared for. I have no wish to frighten you or take advantage of you in any way. And here we are, in this place of luxury. Are you not to enjoy that?"

"Why?"

"Because you should. Because you do matter. Because you are not like other women, not to me. Not like any woman. I am... I am sorry."

He turned away from her and waded out of the bath, walking up out of the tub and grabbing his robe again.

And then he left Agnes sitting there in the water.

CHAPTER SEVEN

AGNES COULD NOT understand what had happened. One moment she had been engaged in… She didn't even know. Some form of seduction at his hands, and the next… Well, the next.

The next he had walked away. She had no idea what her body was doing; her heart felt like it was about to hammer straight out of her chest.

And she was… She was disappointed. She was angry. She couldn't countenance why. Except that she had wanted his mouth on hers again. And on other places. And she felt restless and unsettled for having not gotten it. She should not feel this way.

She didn't know what was happening with Lazarus. A man who was usually… He was usually so easy to read. He was a man of great integrity. And therefore his actions tended to be deliberate. Never random, never…

But he had been like a wild beast these last few days and she… Her heart couldn't take it. She loved him. And she had tried very hard to put that love in its proper place. But now the things that he'd done... It indicated that he desired her. But did he? She couldn't read him and she had no idea what he was playing at. If she was the one who mattered or not. And how would she ever know?

She knew Lazarus. When they traveled, she slept at his feet in the woods, making sure to be the one who kept guard over his body. She had pledged herself. Her heart, her life, to him. And he took care of her. Something that she knew he took great pride in, but that was not the same as feelings.

She had never actually seen an indication that Lazarus had feelings. Loving him was like loving rock. And she had resigned herself to that. Maybe that was sad.

It was why in the end she had said she needed to leave. Because if he didn't care, if he did not feel bonded to her, if he did not feel like he needed her, then what was there?

But then he had... The way that he had looked coming toward her in the bath.

Her treacherous body betrayed her even now. Her nipples were tight, and the place between her legs was wet and sore.

She would never forget the sight of him. Naked and well muscled. She had never seen a naked man in person before. And of course it should be him. Lazarus.

The very first man she'd ever seen naked.

The muscles on his body were like art. The lines and ridges there a testament to his perfection.

And his… His masculinity.

Thick and large and hard for her.

For you?

Because he had walked away, and if he could walk away… Did it really matter? Did she? She swam farther into the bath, trying to get away from the site of her own weakness.

What would become of her if she wasn't with him?

She couldn't imagine a life, she couldn't imagine herself without him, and that was terrifying. She didn't know what manner of creature she was if she was not in Lazarus's care. And there had been a time when she had been… When she had been alone in the world and she'd had to make her own way. She had tried so hard to forget that. But maybe by doing that she had made herself far too dependent. Because he could break her. He could break her and he was on the verge of it, and she did not know what to do about that.

She lay there in the water, floating. And she wondered about herself. Then she submerged herself beneath the water and tried not to think anymore. It didn't help. Certainly wouldn't fix the gnawing ache in her soul.

* * *

A few things had become clear to Lazarus while he had set about making sure that the dinner would be to Agnes's standards. The first was that he must seduce her. However he could. The second was that once he did so, he would make her his wife in truth, not just in a showy way for his brother. No. He did not have time to be thinking of this now, and he knew it, but Agnes was forcing things to a crisis point, as was his newfound desire for her.

And perhaps it was because she had threatened to leave. Perhaps it was because she was abandoning him.

You said you did not need her.

He didn't. He could protect himself just as well. He had no actual need of Agnes. And that was the strangest thing of all. He was not a man that clung to the things that were superfluous. But Agnes did not feel superfluous. Not in any manner. Rather she felt significant.

But then…

He felt a bond to Agamemnon, long dead though he was, and a responsibility to him, because he had saved his life. And while he would not consider himself a spiritualist in the sense that the people of the wood were, while he did not necessarily literally believe in spirits and fae inhabiting the trees, he could not deny that there did seem to be a spiritual connection inherent in the saving of a life. Lazarus had few connections in his life.

Agnes was the one who remained.

And so perhaps it was not wholly without merit to keep her with him.

He needed a wife eventually. Particularly if he were going to rule Liri in the fashion that monarchs did. The idea made him extremely uncomfortable. He was not a man who craved power. He was not a man who wanted it. But in order to do what needed to be done, he would have to take it. And that meant he would need a Queen. And she would need to bear him heirs.

He had thought of finding himself a soft, lovely princess who had been raised to expect such a fate.

But a woman such as that wouldn't be able to handle all that he was, and in many ways Agnes had been in training to be by his side for the last eight years. She could share his bed as well. Get round with his child.

The idea made heat run through his veins.

He stood for a long moment, at the beautifully appointed table on the balcony where Agnes would meet him soon. And he tried to think of when exactly his feelings for her had changed.

Perhaps it was just basic male need.

The desire for a bedmate that could match him. He had not yet found one.

Agnes was his match in battle, and maybe on

some level he had always known he was training her for his bed.

No. He had not.

He thought back to her, scared and wide-eyed in the alley in Paris.

He had not felt those things for her then, but one thing he had known was that she would be in his life forever. And he had turned to walk away. He had tried then to break that bond that Agamemnon had told him existed between two people when a life was saved.

"Where are you going?"

"Back to my kingdom."

"Can I go with you?"

And he could remember regarding her then. And wondering what on earth he was going to do with a girl such as her. She was so small. Frail almost.

Her black hair was dull, her expression one of a near permanent frown.

What could be done with her? What could be done with such a creature?

He had taken her back against his better judgment, and they had begun to train. And that sense of confusion as to why she was with him faded as he saw her improve. As her hair became glossy and her petite frame became strengthened by muscle. As her coordination grew and her speed and sense of timing became unerring.

She was a glory. This girl.

Get up to 4
FREE FABULOUS BOOKS
You Love!

To thank you for being a loyal reader we'd like to send you up to 4 FREE BOOKS, absolutely free.

Just write "YES" on the Loyal Reader Voucher and we'll send you up to 4 Free Books and Free Mystery Gifts, altogether worth over $20, as a way of saying thank you for being a loyal reader.

Try **Harlequin® Desire** books featuring the worlds of the American elite with juicy plot twists, delicious sensuality and intriguing scandal.

Try **Harlequin Presents®** Larger-print books featuring the glamourous lives of royals and billionaires in a world of exotic locations, where passion knows no bounds.

Or **TRY BOTH!**

We are so glad you love the books as much as we do and can't wait to send you great new books.

So don't miss out, return your Loyal Reader Voucher Today!

Pam Powers

LOYAL READER
FREE BOOKS VOUCHER

▲ If offer card is missing write to: Harlequin Reader Service, P.O. Box 1341, Buffalo, NY 14240-8531 or visit www.ReaderService.com ▲

BUSINESS REPLY MAIL
FIRST-CLASS MAIL   PERMIT NO. 717   BUFFALO, NY

POSTAGE WILL BE PAID BY ADDRESSEE

HARLEQUIN READER SERVICE
PO BOX 1341
BUFFALO NY 14240-8571

NO POSTAGE
NECESSARY
IF MAILED
IN THE
UNITED STATES

And then she had become… Inevitable.

She was with him when he needed to make decisions. She was a constant. As though she were part of him in a way that no one and nothing had ever been.

And only a few weeks ago, she had been tending the fire at the camp, and the flame had caught her expression, lit up her smile, her skin a golden glow in the light.

And he had known then that he could use her for this. To be the woman by his side when he came into Liri. And truly, he had realized there could be no other.

So why did he think there could be another in truth? There couldn't be. It would have to be her. And so, he would give her what she needed. For had she not told him exactly what it was? To be special. To be in an exalted position, while he could give her that. And why not? It made sense.

She had come from a gutter, from such an unstable life. It was understandable in the extreme that she should want something better for herself as she made a life going forward. And perhaps he would not have to let her go at all. Perhaps she did not need an education outside of him if he were to expand her knowledge.

It was then that she appeared out on the balcony. Wrapped in that gold gown that had been chosen back at the store in Paris. She was an exquisite thing. And he wished to devour her.

She looked at him, with deep suspicion on her beautiful face. "This is for show?"

"It is for you," he said.

"For me?"

"Yes. It was set up for show, yes. So that my brother would think that we are together. But it is more than that." He pulled her chair out, and she crossed the space, pausing in front of it. "Will you not sit?"

She did so, looking up at him with wonder on her face.

"A second fine dining experience in only a week, it is very strange."

"You want to have these things. Don't you think?"

"I don't think there's anything I ought to have. I have a great deal more than I ever expected to. Stability and home and… I suppose that will change when all of this is over. You will be here."

"Perhaps. Or perhaps I will move the seat of power into the wood."

"How will you rule if the people cannot see you?"

He laughed. "I don't know. But I never feel uncertain for long. Eventually it becomes clear."

"You're very confident."

"Of course. Have I not always been right?"

"Were you right down in the baths?"

She was baiting him. He should've expected nothing less from Agnes. "Yes," he said. "I was right to leave you because you were uncertain. If there is to be sex between us, Agnes, then you must want it."

Her face turned red. Like a beet. It was not delicate, and it was… Surprisingly female. In a way that he found appealing.

"I never said I wish there to be. Or that I didn't. I… I found it overwhelming."

"And then you are not sure. Sex should not be something you are uncertain about. It should be something you cannot go without. Something you cannot deny. The decision should be made with your body. And once your body is in the space of being able to make that decision for you… Then it is clear. There is no place for uncertainty, not then."

It became clear to him then what he wanted from Agnes. The next surrender. She had sworn her life to him out of obligation. Now he wanted her to beg for him in desperation. And he could make her do that. Of this he was sure. And it was what he desired above all else. Seduction.

That would make her his. He had her with him all this time, and he had failed to see what it was she actually desired. He would not fail there again.

"And now we eat."

The food was exactly as he had instructed. Perfectly made and exquisitely presented. Heavy on the sweets.

There was an array of cakes for dessert, in addition to rich chocolate truffles and lovely cream pies. Anything, essentially, that his Agnes could desire.

"Tell me about Ohio," he said.

Agnes laughed. "That is something that… No one has ever said to me."

"Will you tell me?"

"I will. What little I remember." Her lips turned down. "You know, I don't remember anything. I remember the house. Two story, but not fine. It was drafty in the winter. Sometimes the power was turned off. I remember my mother, but never smiling. And then… Well, and then I remember her funeral. Not many people came. I think her parents were there, what would be my grandparents. But they didn't stay, and they didn't talk to my father. They didn't seem to want to know me.

"I remember my father said they came from Hawaii. So they were cold. It was Ohio and it was winter. I don't know. That's all I remember. And then we started to move. My father said that he had a business opportunity and we were going to fly on a plane. And I had never done that before. After that we got on a very long flight. And I had one bag. From there on out we spent my childhood moving around Europe. We started in Germany. Then went to England. Luxembourg. Belgium. We were in Switzerland for a while. Then Norway. I loved it there. It was beautiful and wild. We spent time in Iceland, which I also loved. And along the way I picked up bits of all those languages. I forgot everything about my life before. At least, as much as I could. And I just sort of lived. Whatever reality, whatever moment we were in. It was easier. Easier to forget that I had ever gone to a real school. Easier to forget that I had a mother. That I had grandparents somewhere. It was all just easier. My father ran cons wherever we were. Sometimes with the aid of other people, which was why we would move. Or sometimes the law would close in on us and we would have to leave. I had no less than six passports before I was ten."

So strong. So brave. He had been too late. Would that he'd been there to save her then.

"That is no kind of life," he said, his voice rough.

"It was the only one I knew. Then we went to Paris. Which… At fifteen felt very exciting. But it began to wear on me quickly. It's a beautiful city. But like any place… There's an underside, and it is often bleak. Grim. All of the glamour and glitter on the top is just that. You take too deep of a breath and you blow it all away, and you just have the grime beneath. But I still loved walking to the Eiffel Tower. Gazing up at it. And I would take what little money I had, then buy myself bread and sit there. And imagine what it would be like if there was someone… Anyone who could take me away from that life. And then you came. And you rescued me when everything seemed lost. I'm grateful to you for that forever."

He could not help himself. He reached out and pressed his thumb to her cheek, only for a moment. Agnes, warm and alive and his.

She had sworn loyalty to him from the first, but this was different.

Entirely different.

"I don't know that I deserve gratitude for doing what anyone should have."

"Many people would have had to call the police. There would've been no other choice. They could not have single-handedly destroyed all those men and protected me."

"Well, that is down to my upbringing. In the end, we are all that we are created," he said.

"Until we are shown a different way. You took me away from the life that I knew. And you made me something different. Like I told you, I used to think about nothing. Just a moment. And every so often I would dream. But that was it. I didn't dwell on the things that were around me because they were… I knew that I didn't want to steal people's money, but I didn't know what else to do. I knew that I didn't want to be a con man, and I knew that I didn't think what my father did was right. But find-ing a way out was hard, and I couldn't see it. So I

took my thoughts away, and I just did my best to not
have them. It is not the best way to live. It is not. I
think we are all what we are shown until someone
gives us the strength, the insight, into something
new. Until we are safe enough to want more. That's
what you gave to me."

"Do you remember your last name?"

She shook her head. "No. I don't like to go that
deep. I'm sure it's there, somewhere. I must've written it on assignments at school. But it's just been
so long."

"And it's part of a person you wish to forget."

"Yes."

She looked around. "I cannot imagine being back
at my childhood home. What is it like for you?"

He looked around at the expansive, beautiful terrace.

His childhood home. Such an odd thing to call
a palace, and yet it was true.

But he had been four years old when he'd left,
and Agnes had been more like six. So perhaps that
two years carried with it more memories than the
previous four could have.

And yet… And yet.

He let his mind go to the watercolor past, which
was blurred and beautifully colored, but nothing
distinct. But it carried with it feelings, like a paint-
ing by a master. The meaning could be unclear, but
the emotion was not.

And for the first time he let himself stay in it. Stare at it. Marvel at it.

"What I have are vague pictures. Vague impressions of a time when I was here, more than... More than real memories."

"Do you remember your room?"

"I carry a picture of it. In my head. And I remember lying beneath the covers of the bed, and a woman reading to me. Perhaps it was my mother. Perhaps it was a nanny. I'm not sure."

Except he knew it was his mother. Not because he could see her in his mind, but because he could remember the feeling that he had in his chest. Of happiness and contentedness, a sense of well-being that he knew could only, and had only, come from her. He knew this to be true. As sure as he knew anything.

"I remember sitting at the table and having my favorite dinner. It was... Chicken nuggets."

Agnes laughed. "I would never have thought that I might have something in common with a prince. But that was my favorite too. I didn't know they would've made it for you at the palace."

"If I recall correctly I would sit with my brother at a corner of the table opposite my parents, and we were served a different meal."

"Right. Your brother. I didn't have any siblings."

"I didn't either. After I was four."

"Tell me about that day. You have spoken of it, but it's different than telling the story, I think."

"I… I was playing with my brother on the lawn. I remember that. How our ball rolled into the woods and I remember… I remember going after it. And after that I remember it was dark all around me, and I could not see. I thought for sure that the palace was just behind me, but I kept on walking and it wasn't there. I didn't find the ball. I couldn't find my way back home. What seemed dark at first became overwhelmingly pitch-black. And then I began to hear the wolves howl. I knew about the Big Bad Wolf. Always wolves, wolves coming to eat children. Yes, I knew. I knew and I tried to hide. But I could not see. My eyes refused to adjust to that sort of darkness. I wedged myself as far as I could beneath the rock outcropping and slept for a time. And when I woke the sky was gray. I came out, and there they were. A pack of them. And they began to close in on me, and I tried to get back into my safe spot, but it was blocked. They are hunters, and they know how to track their prey.

"And then Agamemnon came. He beat them back with a large stick and set them on their way. He did not kill them. He told me later it was because the people of the wood had learned to exist with the animals. They did not take more than their share—the wolves did not take from the camp. I didn't believe him for a long time, but in all my years there, no one was ever taken by a wolf. But the minute my youngest brother wandered in…"

"Yes," she said. "He was eaten."

Lazarus nodded. "So perhaps there is truth to it. Agamemnon said I was branded as one of them from that moment on. That I was to swear my loyalty to him, and I did. It was easy enough. Easy enough to do. He told me I would have to forget my family. That they could not get me in the wood, and wouldn't. Because my father was afraid to go into it. And then he told me. He told me the story of how my great-grandfather had decided that the native faction of the country was too dangerous. How he had driven them from their homes. How he had demanded they not have their own government anymore. And eventually… They sought solace in the woods, because it was the only way they could escape. But many of them were killed. This was their land. Before explorers came from Greece and established their own hold here. And over the years the cultures mingled, but those that did not…

"Those that did not were always viewed with suspicion. But it was my great-grandfather who decided that it could be no more. That he would stamp out all that made them… Them.

"I was a gift sent to them, Agamemnon said. To right the wrongs that had been done. And it is as you said… You only know what you were raised with until you are shown something else. It is injustice that was done to the people of the forest. And I am the one that was sent to make it right."

"Did Agamemnon never read you stories?"

"No. Not as such. Not tucked into my bed. But he told me tales around the fire. He taught me to hunt and take my own food. Taught me to cook. Taught me to fight. He made me hard, and he made me a man. I went from being a prince who knew how to do nothing but sit at his own corner of the table and eat…chicken nuggets that had been prepared for him. Who spent his days playing ball with his brother… I became a man very quickly. But in the wood there is nothing else."

"Did you ever miss it? Did you miss being a boy?"

"I forgot about it," he said. "Because as you say… It is easier."

And he had not realized that he had quite so much in common with Agnes until that moment. But he hadn't even realized he'd felt that. Hadn't realized it was what he was going to say until just then. But it was true.

"I became something new."

"And you like what you have become?" she asked.

"The man I became is the man that saved you in Paris. The Prince of Liri would not have done that. I'm sure you heard how debauched my brother

Dionysus was. What would've stopped me from becoming such a man?"

"Alex is not that man," Agnes said. "Read anything about him, and you'll see that he is upright, moral. He is very like you, I think."

"So you think. But I'm not convinced."

"And what would it take to convince you?"

"There is nothing," he said. "But it does not matter. We are of one goal, Agnes. And that is justice, yes?"

"I suppose."

"What about… What about in life?"

She tilted her head, looking at him from the corner of her eye, as though she were suspicious. "I have thought little about my life since coming to you. I have not had to. All needs have been met. And like you… I became stronger. I learned to hunt. I learned to fight. If I have to survive, then I can, and I will. And beyond that…"

"You will go off in the world to have experience."

"You're the one who said I should."

"And you are the one who decided it should be permanent. So what is it you dream of?"

CHAPTER EIGHT

AGNES DIDN'T KNOW how to answer that question. Nor did she know what to do with… All of this. For she had never sat and had a conversation with Lazarus as though they were… As though they were friends.

"I once dreamed of safety," she said. "And I found it. I dreamed of always being fed, and you have given me that as well. I'm not certain I know how to dream bigger than that."

"Come now. The girl that went and ate bread at the Eiffel Tower, she did not only dream of bread. What did you dream of?"

"What all people do, I suppose. Yes, I know a great many people dream of jobs. Work and what they will be when they grow up. But those things shift with time, and change. You might want to be an astronaut when you're a child because you don't know how difficult it is to get to the moon. I didn't dream of those things. I did wonder what it would be like, though, to be loved. Not used. But loved. When I dreamed of someone coming to rescue me, I often thought of my grandparents. The ones I never really got to know. Yes, I often thought of them. I just dreamed of what it could be if I… If I found a safe place with people who might open their arms to me. I dreamed of friends."

"A lover?" he pressed.

Her skin flushed, and she remembered, all too well, the heat that Lazarus generated in her body. The truth was she had never dreamed about a lover, not before she met him. Men had always represented something rather frightening. Something foreign and potentially dangerous. And then… Then she had dreamed of a man's touch. Especially when they had begun their training. When he had held her tight and invited her to try to escape him, her whole body had been flushed with heat. And she had not wanted to escape him, not at all, no… She had wanted to lean into him.

She had wanted his hold to change, had wanted his touch to become tender. She… She was so strangely aroused by the man, and then had begun to fall in love with him. Her loyalty had become something different, something deep. But the way that he observed the separation between them had provided safety.

Her hormones had been out of control, he had

spent his own with women closer to his age. Women who were not sad teenagers with terrible crushes.

But still, his calloused hands always made her shiver. And sparring exercises became the most erotic experience in her life.

Until the sword fight in his Parisian penthouse. Until he had…

And then in the baths.

Where she had seen his body. Really.

"Of course I should like one," she said. "I am a warrior, but I am not made of stone. Yes, it has been the easiest thing to devote myself to my training and cast off the idea of having a lover. But… But that is not…is not all I want."

"And so you should leave me and find a man to take as a lover?"

"Perhaps I will," she said, feeling angry now. "Perhaps I shall go off and find myself countless lovers. How many have you had?"

He chuckled. "I do not know the number. Is that what you truly want?"

She wanted him. But it terrified her. She wanted him, and she did not know what to do about that.

She wanted him, but something about it terrified her. Perhaps it was that he was… All things to her. A man of great beauty and consequence. The one who had given her shelter, who had given her purpose. The one who had changed her life.

Perhaps that was why.

He leaned close to her. "I could teach you."

His words were dark and rich like the coffee that she had just drunk with her cake. And the temptation in them was… It was so deep. So real.

"I could show you all the things your body can do, Agnes. But you deserve more than that. More than a simple training."

And now it had gone from temptation into something much, much more dangerous.

"You deserve to have a man take his time with you. To give to you. Has anyone given to you, darling?"

"I… You have given me much."

"I would like to lay you on a soft bed and spend an hour tasting your skin. Every inch of it. I would like to make love to you. Slowly, the first time. But then… You are a warrior. You always were. A woman and a warrior. And I see that. You would not be content only with slow and sweet, would you? You want to sword fight. And I would give it to you. I would test your strength while I held you in my arms. And you would test mine. I want that. Do you know… All of my lovers have been so very soft. I have never had a woman quite like you. And the idea intrigues me. More than intrigues. I want to know what it would be like to take all of your strength and have it pressed against me. Naked. So, this is why it can never be just a training. Because I need you to show me what your body can do.

I need you to show me what mine could do. What it could do only with you. The pleasure I think we might find…"

He was looking at her, and he did not break focus. His words were slow and true, and achingly deliberate. Each one felt like a touch, like that promised caress. Each one felt something like magic. And she wanted it. So very desperately.

She wanted those words to turn into touch. Wanted this moment to turned into more. The pulse at the base of her thighs throbbed, and she could scarcely think past it. Was this why women made whole fools of themselves after men? She had seen women do it at the camp. Giggling after Lazarus. Wanting so badly for him to turn his attentions to them. But he did not have time for the giggly ones. He preferred experienced women, at least he always had. An observation she had made. And one that made her feel even more like she was in her own category.

But he had said… He had said that he had never wanted a woman like her before. That he had never been with one.

And that was the greatest temptation of all. He leaned across the space, and he touched her lips to his.

And her body caught fire.

His kiss was achingly slow, deliberate. But not for show, not like the one in the restaurant. He parted her lips with his tongue and tasted her deep, and she became lost in the slick rhythm. Lost in the feel of his mouth on hers like so.

His kisses made her feel drugged. And she slowly began to lose all resistance. All worries. Because there was nothing but this. Nothing but that large calloused hand on her face, stroking her rather than holding her for a fight. His mouth was not issuing commands, but rather demanding response with each pass of his lips over hers.

This was more dangerous than any battle she had ever engaged in, and she was going into it willingly. With all that she had in her. She was so desperate and wet between her legs, needy for something she knew only he could give.

Hadn't he given it to her once? The touch of his tongue on her most intimate flesh.

The kiss he had given her there would reverberate inside of her for the rest of her life.

And how much more so if he took possession of her? With that thick, glorious male member of his that she had seen for the first time in the baths.

She had been afraid then.

Because she had felt like he wanted her... Well, she didn't know why. He had been angry. She could see that. Angry, and his touch had been a demand in a way that had frightened and confused her.

But this was different.

This was different.

She found herself pressing as near to him as she could without falling off of her chair, and then he wrapped his arms around her waist and pulled her directly to his chair, bringing her legs on either side of his, placing the heart of her directly in contact with that hardest part of him. And she gasped. And found herself moving her hips in a sensuous rhythm that she somehow simply knew, even though she had never done anything like this before.

She just knew.

Her body knew exactly what it was required to do. And she was chasing pleasure. Chasing the desire that he aroused in her with all the intensity that she possessed in her soul. An intensity created by her time with Lazarus. For before she had been soft. Before she had been nothing more than a leaf drifting on the wind. And now she created the wind. All because of him.

And together… Together they were making a storm.

She cupped his face, kissing him back, deep and hard and with all of the longing inside of her. She rocked her hips against his arousal, gasping as he hit that spot that was so aroused with desire for him.

Oh, how she wanted to feel him there. Hard and thick, surging within her, and even though the idea frightened her, those virginal nerves that few could ever outrun, she also needed it. Craved it. Desired it above all else.

"Lazarus," she whispered.

"Yes?"

"Lazarus, I…"

"You can still speak," he said, dragging his thumb down her face. "That means I have not done a good enough job."

She wanted to protest. He had done a fine job. She was gasping with her need for him. Desperate.

"Tonight, I think you shall sleep, Agnes. And you will not be bothered by me."

Bothered. She was not bothered. Well, she was bothered. Rather warm with it.

But she wanted…

"I want you desperate, darling."

"Darling?"

He had called her that about twice.

"Agnes," he said, in that way only he did. "Darling Agnes."

And she did not know what to do now, for he set her back in her chair, and she felt unsatisfied and confused. He had said that when it came to sex you had to be mindless and not in control, but he still was. Or he would not have stopped it. She would not have stopped. She would have let him take her there on the terrace. She would not have been able to control herself.

And why did he want her now?

That thought pounded in her head while she sat

there and finished the last slice of her cake. And again as they made their way to their bedchamber.

"Lazarus? What do you want with me?"

"I have been giving it a great deal of thought, Agnes," he said. "And I think… Yes, I said that I wanted you to see the world. I stand by that. You should have some experience away from me. But… When you return I want you to be my wife."

CHAPTER NINE

AGNES COULD NOT believe what she was hearing. He wanted her to be his wife?

"What do you need a wife for?"

"I'm to be King. I will need a wife. And I will need heirs. You are… You are bound to me in a way that I cannot explain. And now I think I understand it. This is what was always meant to be. I could never have a soft princess by my side. I need a warrior. It is built into my blood. On the deepest level of who I am. That is what I require."

And then he disappeared into the bath chamber, and she heard the water running for the shower a moment later.

She sat on the edge of the bed, her pulse pounding heavily. He wanted her to be his wife. He wanted her to be his wife because she made sense.

But with that she would have… She would have a permanent place by his side, and there would be no other women. And for Agnes, who had never done much dreaming, it was…

But it was not about love.

And she had dreamed of love once.

But you know how the world works. It is not so simple. Neither was it half so wonderful as she'd once dreamed.

It was true. How could one woman ever hope to have all of those things? A place in Lazarus's heart and by his side. Ample food and shelter.

But he's bent on revenge…

He was. And he would say it wasn't revenge, he would say that it was…

But there was more. He spoke of his family, and they were not bad memories. And yet something in him was twisted in regard to them, and it wasn't just the stories that Agamemnon had told him. She could sense that.

Inside of him was a frightened boy whose father had not found him. It was another man who had saved him from the jaws of the wolves.

It wasn't true that they had never really looked for him? Was it true they had not done so because of what had happened generations before with the people of the forest?

She wondered. And if she wondered, then he certainly did. He certainly did.

She sat, and she waited. And decided what she was going to do.

And there was only one conclusion she could come to.

That his seduction at the table was more calculated than he would have her think. And she had to test it. If this was a battle, then she would have to pick up her sword. If this was a battle, then she would have to test herself in truth. And test him.

And there was only one way to do so.

You should be mindless.

You should be unable to stop.

Agnes stood slowly from the edge of the bed and crossed the space to the wardrobe where her things had been put. Everything that she had tried on at the Parisian fashion boutique, and many things she had not.

And she was gratified by what she found.

There was an outfit—it could be called that— made entirely of gold lace. Open up the front, with a belt at the waist, and a pair of the tiniest undergarments she had ever seen. Just for the lower half.

She stripped all of her clothing off and put it on. And examined herself in the mirror. She could see the shadow of dark hair between her thighs through the underwear. Could see the dusky hint of her nipples beneath the lace of the dress.

And he would see them as well. But he had seen her naked already, so why not this?

Why not?

And she waited. Waited for him to emerge again.

And when he did, he had nothing but a towel wrapped around his waist, his glorious torso gleaming in the golden light, water droplets rolling down his chest, rippling over his ab muscles. He was a truly beautiful man. The most beautiful that she had ever seen.

And will you regret this?

No. The answer came, swift and simple. Whatever happened after this, she would not regret it.

Because there were only two possible outcomes. He would pass her test, and she would agree to be his wife. She would. It was that simple. Or he would fail and... Well then, she would remain a virgin. And she would go on into her new life and find another lover. One who was mindless for her.

"Agnes," he said, his voice rough.

He was not unaffected.

"As we have discussed," she said. "You are not my King any longer. I do not have to follow your every order."

"Do you not?" His voice was deceptively calm. But she knew him well enough to know that a person could not have any sort of false sense of security when it came to Lazarus.

"You stopped things before I was ready."

"You don't know what you're ready for."

"You cannot help it. You say that you do not wish to be my teacher, but you cannot help it. But sex,

Lazarus, requires two people to be desperate. To be mindless. And you think far too much."

She walked toward him, and she tried to remember the way those other women moved. Slow and sensuous, with a rock in their hips, their breasts thrust out into prominence. Yes, she tried to think of that and keep her gaze on his. And a surge of power went through her when she realized he could not take his eyes off her. He was waiting to see what she would do next, and he did not know. She did not know what she would do either, but she was gratified that she was able to surprise him.

Even if she would have to surprise herself, and make decisions very quickly.

And when she reached him, it seemed obvious. She did exactly what she wanted to. She wanted to touch that great and glorious chest, for she always had. For he was incredible and beautiful in all ways, and she had lusted after his body since before she understood exactly what it was she was feeling.

She could remember clearly the first night she had understood that she desired him the way that a woman desired a man. It had been when a woman had approached him at the campfire, all curves and heavy-lidded smiles.

She had put her hand on his chest, and Lazarus had responded, taking her hand and going off with her into the darkness.

And that was when she had realized exactly what

they did in the darkness. And when she had imagined putting her hand on his chest. When she had imagined what might happen if she were to touch him that way. And what it would be like if he led her off into the darkness. What then? She felt sick with jealousy but things had made sense then. In a way they had not before, and in some ways she was grateful for it. Because it had given her clarity. And so there was that. But it had eaten at her as well.

And so she did it now.

Touched his chest.

She had wanted to then. As she had wanted to do since she was just seventeen and falling desperately in love with him, while understanding slowly what that meant. How impossible it was.

In some ways, though, she had been happy. Because at least she had felt love. Even if it wasn't returned. She had loyalty. But now… Now she could touch him, as a woman touched a man. Now she could reach down into those hidden parts of herself. The woman, not the warrior. The woman who had sworn so much more to him than fealty, but had sworn her heart.

And now she would swear her body to him, if he would have it.

And you will extract all the desire in his whole being from him.

She knew it then. For perhaps what he'd said was true. And he had really never had a woman like her.

And yes, it was to be her first time.

But she did not want gentle. She wanted them. What they were.

Not what someone else might be. Not how he would handle a virgin, but how he would handle Agnes.

Hand flat, splayed over his chest, she moved it down his body boldly, taking in the sensation of his muscles, of the crisp hair there that was so different from anything on her own body. He was a man. And there was no denying it. And she was a woman.

Often with them those lines blurred, because they were warriors, but here in this space it was undeniable. Here in this space, they were one. And, too, such very different entities all at the same time.

"I want you," she said. "Do you know how much? How unfair it was when you put your mouth on me when I was not prepared after spending years working to banish the fantasies that I had of you? It was nearly impossible to endure. And then you… Then you changed everything. You changed everything when you put your mouth on mine, and when you put your mouth…there. On that secret place where I've… I've tried not to want you. And you think of me as innocent, I know you do, but my fantasies of you have not been innocent. Not for a very long time."

And then she pushed her hand down beneath the edge of the towel, which loosened the knot, and she saw it falling to the floor. And his body was exposed to her. Oh, his body. It was so beautiful. So incredibly beautiful.

"I want you," she repeated, and she wrapped her fingers around his thick length, around the evidence that he was just as desperate for her as she was for him.

He groaned, harsh and short, his breath hissing through his teeth. His eyes closed and his head fell back, and she had never seen him... She had never seen him like this. There was a resignation in the action that was nothing like the Lazarus she had known these last eight years.

She felt powerful. Holding him like this. And breathless with desire. It was the strangest thing. To feel both strong and weak all at once. Like she could do anything, and like he could defeat her were he to place his lips on hers and kiss her until she was mindless.

But they were locked in a battle where both would emerge victorious in the end.

A thrill of excitement raced through her.

"Do I please you?" she asked, lifting her eyes to his, and then following some instinct she hadn't known she possessed, drawing her tongue across her upper lip.

And that was when he moved. He gripped her wrists, propelling her backward, and taking her down onto the bed, his naked body looming over hers.

"Little witch," he said.

"Perhaps," she said. "This feels a bit like magic." And then she arched herself upward, and she could feel him respond. Could feel his powerlessness to do anything but meet her there. His desire as intense and terrifying as her own. And then, with all the strength she possessed, she wrapped her leg around his waist and reversed their positions, so that she was on top of him, looking down at his glorious naked form. She put her hands to the belt on the dress, letting the fabric fall loose, and then shrugging the gold film from her shoulders, letting it fall so that she was bare breasted above him.

"Is this a fight for dominance then?" he asked, his voice silky. "Because I warn you. I will win."

She thought of how strong he was. The glory she would feel in such a defeat. "I think we would both win in that case."

He growled again, and she found herself flat on her back, her panties being ripped from her body. "Do not play with me."

"This is not a game," she said. "You were treating me as if I were game. A quarry. Something to be snared and caught, and you were so controlled. You had me begging for you, and you would not give me what I wanted. This is no place for games. Not you and me. Either we need to have each other, or we don't have each other at all."

The growl intensified, and he gripped her hands,

lacing his fingers through hers as he pressed them down into the mattress. "Can you handle the manner of my need?"

"I know nothing else," she said. "Are we not a product of the environment wherein we were shaped and created? Because I was shaped in your world, Lazarus. Honed into the thing you see before you by your own hand. Were you not always making yourself a bedmate?"

Something flashed through his eyes, and she knew that she had bested him. Yet again.

He said nothing, instead he lowered his head and kissed her, the gesture a punishment that she was more than willing to take.

She could feel his heart raging in his chest, raging out of control.

And then she knew, yet again, exactly what she would do next. She pulled away from him, scattering kisses down his chest, and then she wiggled out from beneath him, and he moved so as to catch her, and she took that opportunity to bring herself back to him, kissing his stomach, the hard ridges of his ab muscles, all the way down to where he was hard and thick for her.

Because why should he be the only one who could undo her?

She put her mouth on him, then opened her lips around the thick head of him, drawing him in as deeply as she could.

His hand went to her hair, gripping her tightly as he swore violently and she didn't stop. He didn't make her. And he could have.

Just as she could've made him stop when he had eaten into her in the Parisian penthouse. And she had not. Because the desire was too strong. Because the need for release was greater than the need for sanity.

Mindless.

Desperate.

How they knew it well. She pleasured him like that, until he was shaking, until his hands in her hair were nearly beyond pain. And then he wrenched her away from him, brought her back up his body and kissed her. Then those rough, large hands were between her thighs, stroking her, taking her to the brink, before bringing her back again.

"Please," she whimpered. "Lazarus, please."

"Beg me," he growled.

"Lazarus…"

"Beg me for your release."

"Please," she said again.

"Please what?"

"My Lord," she said. "Please."

And then he moved his hand just so and gave her exactly what she had needed. Exactly what she had been longing for. Desire broke over her like so many scattered stars, her release of fractured glass pane cracking all around her.

And when she came back to herself, he was there, over her, the thick blunt tip of him pressed against the entrance to her body.

"This may hurt," he growled, and then in the next moment he thrust home, swallowing her gasp of pain with a kiss.

And it was only pain.

Pain existed only to the degree that you allowed it, something she had learned in her training. And she let it fall away. She made it so that it did not matter. Pain was immaterial. What mattered was that he was inside of her. Connected to her. Closer than she had ever been to another person.

Lazarus. Him.

And then he began to move, taking those pieces of pain and replacing them, thrust by thrust, with pleasure that ran deep.

Until she was sobbing, gasping with it.

Until she was begging him for more. For everything.

Until she was poised on that brink once again, that shattering place that only he had ever really brought her to.

And when it burst, it was all glitter. And there was nothing dark or insidious beneath. It was bright all the way down, the kind of glory that she had only ever dreamed existed in this world.

And when he shattered right along with her, it was like dying and being made new again.

Mindless. Desperate.

No different than her. It was not a game, or a manipulation. Or a means to an end. Not for her either. It was just beyond her. Beyond them.

And then Agnes, who had not shed a single tear even when her father had been killed in an alley in Paris, began to cry.

CHAPTER TEN

LAZARUS LOOKED DOWN at the trembling woman in his arms. His Agnes.

And he… He could not recall the last time he had completely lost the plot like that. He never had. That was why he could not remember it. Because the moment did not exist. She had taken his plans and twisted them, made it so he could not even remember the aim of his seduction. And she had turned it into her seduction. And he had… He had succumbed. Quickly. Willingly.

Were you not always making yourself a bedmate?

And now she was weeping. This woman who had come toward him with such strength and power was shattered in his arms, crying like a child. And he did not know what to do.

He was comfortable dealing with battle. Comfortable dealing with a fight. But this… This moment was out of his reach. He did not know what to do. He did not know what it made him. There had been a time in his life when someone had tucked him in and read him bedtime stories. But it was not now. And it had not been for a very long time. There had been softness in his life, but he could not remember it. And yet he held her up against his chest, because it seemed the right thing to do, whether he fully understood or not. He felt like there was a large space between them, and he did not know how he might cross it. He did not know if it were possible.

"Why…why are you crying?" he asked.

She pressed her cheek against him, wet from her tears getting on his skin. "I don't know."

"Have I hurt you?"

"No," she said on a jagged sigh. "I'm not injured."

"Then I do not understand."

"I don't either." She looked up at him, her eyes shining bright. "It is okay to not understand, Lazarus."

No. It wasn't. He was a man who did not traffic in unknowns. But rather in the things that he could see and touch. And he had been proud of this. For much of this time. He had… It made sense. The things that were tangible. That he could see and touch and taste. And beyond that… Beyond that none of it mattered. At least, he had thought so. Until he lay there with this woman, holding her, trying to make sense of what she was feeling. And of why he wanted so badly to protect her when there was no threat.

"You don't like this," she said. "Because it was not your timing."

"God laughed at my timing," he said wryly.

And it was true. He had sought to control her with desire, and she had turned it around on him, as a blade wielded sloppily by an enemy who had underestimated his foe.

He had underestimated her. And he had underestimated his desire for her. But perhaps... Perhaps because she had desired him this whole time, perhaps because she had known... Perhaps that was why she had managed to best him so effectively.

She was acquainted with this desire between them while he... It was new to him. Or at least, the understanding of it. But he had not known.

"You have wanted me?" he asked.

She nodded. "You are the only honorable man I have ever known. I honestly wasn't sure if I had any use for men until I met you. And you... You are so brave and steady. And you put your life at risk to save mine. So yes, I wanted you. But in every way. To wish to keep me in your life, to approve of me. To hold on to me. And I knew... I knew when I saw the way those women touched you that I wished I could touch you the same. But I... I also knew that I would never do anything that would make you want to send me away. That I would never do anything that would make me any less to you than I was. And so I determined that I would be Agnes. The most and best, the one who swore everything to you. And if that meant being chased, that I would be. For my desire was tied to you anyway."

"Agnes," he said, feeling unequal to the declaration in the moment. "There is no other one like you."

And then she settled her head against his chest. "And there is none like you."

There was something in that statement. Something in that declaration that soothed a beast inside of him he had not known was roaring there.

He wanted to keep her, but not in the same way he'd felt compelled to do so before. This was not about holding hard, but gentle. Keeping her in contact with him, his skin, but not holding so tight as to trap her, to crush her.

He just wanted to hold her.

And so he did. And whatever happened next, he would meet at the head then. But for now, Agnes was soothed, she had stopped crying and she was in his arms. Everything else would take care of itself.

The next morning Agnes was invited to tea with Tinley. It was a very frightening request, all things considered. She had just been with Lazarus for the first time, the way women and men were, and they were lying to Tinley and Alexius. She felt a jumble of nerves as she walked into the future Queen's personal sitting area, which was lovely and well-appointed.

"Good afternoon," she said.

"Agnes," Tinley said, smiling broadly. "You look…well."

But she could tell the way that Tinley said that meant she did not. Agnes blinked.

"Is there something wrong with me?"

"No," Tinley said. "There's nothing wrong with you. Why would you think that?"

"You look very disconcerted."

"It's only that you look sort of pale."

Great. So everything that had happened with Lazarus was written all over her.

"I'm fine. I'm very much looking forward to tea. You know I really like desserts."

"Lazarus has said. You don't suppose there's a chance you could be pregnant."

She felt her eyes go wide. And the truth of the matter was… She and Lazarus had done nothing to prevent such a thing. They hadn't even thought of it. Or discussed it. It hadn't crossed her mind even once. But technically, she would not be pregnant yet. "I… Likely not. It's fine."

"And is everything well with you and Lazarus?"

"I… Yes," she said. "We are well. Lazarus is a hard man, but he is good," Agnes said.

"And you love him," Tinley said. "Please sit down. I'll pour you some tea."

This was that female heart-to-heart sort of thing that Tinley wanted to have. And Agnes had never engaged in. She had always been hiding things about herself. And right now it was no different. She was hiding.

"Lazarus saved my life," Agnes said. "Literally. I was a girl on the streets of Paris, and he... He undoubtedly saved me from a very grim fate. I have loved him since I was sixteen years old."

"Sometimes that isn't love," Tinley said. "And I don't say that to be discouraging. It's only that... Agnes, I have some experience with that. I thought I loved Dionysus very much. I couldn't sort out the feelings that I had for Alexius. Until... Until much later. What I felt for Dionysus was not love. It was just a childish sort of infatuation."

"I'm not infatuated with Lazarus," Agnes said, laughing. As if that word could be applied to the two of them. The sword fights and sparring. The way that he talked to her. The way that he touched her. It was nothing half so simple as infatuation. If only it could be. "I love him," Agnes said. "But there is... An intensity to that."

Tinley laughed then, a high, pleasant-sounding sound. "Well, if you had a late night, you should've simply said that."

"Yes," Agnes said. "A very late night. Thank you

for the romantic meal, and the time at the baths. I…
I very much think that it… Enhanced that."

She felt uncomfortable sharing so much, even
though she was only sort of playing a part. But
was she? And now Lazarus wanted her to be his
wife in truth. So what did that mean. What did any
of it mean.

"He and Alexius are going riding today," Tinley said. "Brotherly bonding. You have no idea how
much Alexius has felt… Lazarus's loss weighed
heavily on him. For all of his life."

Guilt started to chew at Agnes.

"The loss of both of his brothers… It's been a
shadow over him. Over his life. It took a lot to get
him to where he is now. And he… He really is wonderful."

"Lazarus is not an easy man. Because he didn't
have an easy time. Life in the wood is not easy. It's
very difficult, and he had to figure out a way to survive. As a young boy who lost his family the way
that he did. And in his mind, he did lose them. As
soon as he was in the wood, he was beyond their
reach. He… He doesn't know softness."

And neither did Agnes. Not really.

"And you? He saved you and brought you into
the forest? How has that been for you?"

"Good. As long as I've been with him."

And it was true. She was happy when she was
with him. So why couldn't they be together. Re-

ally be together. He had proposed marriage, and she knew that it had nothing to do with love. Not for him. But she did love him. It was the true thing that bonded her to him, not honor, not anything else. Perhaps that was enough. Perhaps it could be enough.

One thing she knew, the sooner they finished here the better. She did not like lying to Tinley. And she did not know how to reconcile her feelings for Lazarus with the growing discomfort over what it was he planned for their hosts.

For there was more to that man she loved than revenge. She knew it.

But she did not know if she could ever make him believe it.

CHAPTER ELEVEN

"A GOOD DAY to ride," Alexius said, as they reached the top of the mountain and looked down over the castle, over the wood, over everything.

"Yes," Lazarus agreed. For while he might have to be guarded around his brother, he would not lie about something so obvious. It was a good day for a ride.

"What do you see when you look at it?"

Lazarus glanced at his brother. "I'm sorry, I don't understand."

"The kingdom. What do you see when you look down upon it. Do you see your home? Or is the wood your home?"

"That is a complicated question," Lazarus said.

"I had a sense that it was. I'm trying to understand, from you, Lazarus, what it is you wish."

"Why do you think I wish anything?"

"Because you're not a man of inaction. And yet you have been sitting in the palace enjoying my hospitality and… And that's all. Your fiancée is lovely, and I heard that you greatly enjoyed the dinner that was set out for you, and I'm pleased to hear that. But I wonder… I do wonder if there is more. More that you want. More that you need."

And this was the moment then. To speak. To state his intent. And above all else, Lazarus was a man of honor. And so while it was one thing to sit and engage in some manner of subterfuge without speaking of what it was he wanted, he would not lie. Not directly. He would give his brother a chance to face him head-on. And he would do so now.

"What do you know the history of Liri?"

"As much as any schoolchild. But undoubtedly more. Our father made certain that I knew everything."

"And yet you did not know there was a kingdom in the woods."

"No," Alexius said, his voice faltering. "I did not."

"And have you asked yourself why that is? Why he would want to keep it a secret. Why it would not be spoken of widely. Why is it that none of you living in this kingdom know that there was another kingdom within it?"

"I don't know," he said.

"They stole this land. You know that this place was settled broadly by Greeks, Italians, others from that region of Europe."

"Yes. There was a lot of land and ample opportunity here."

"Yes. A great and vast wilderness. And what became of that? It was tamed. And what happened to the people who lived here first?"

"I confess that I don't know."

"They went into the woods, Alexius. And there they have waited. For something. For justice of some kind. And I have been charged with ensuring that justice is done."

"And what, to you, is justice?"

"My people were driven from their homes. They were driven from this land. They have no say in this government. They do not have the ruling body they once had. For our great-grandfather… He was threatened by it."

"Tell me everything. Show me everything. Lazarus, I will not stand by and let injustice be done. If there's one thing I've always been certain of, it's that our family was cursed. Two brothers going to the woods and neither come out? There's a reason for that. There has to be. There has always had to be. It's a punishment. And I'm certain of it.

"This history is a blight on our family," Alex said. "I want… I want to do something to fix it."

"Do you?" And Lazarus could not pinpoint quite why he had imagined his brother would be a villain in this. Except… Except. He had not wanted to think that anyone in his family could be anything more than that. On some level he had wanted to be-lieve that the only way to be true, the only way to be good, was to stick to that Spartan life he'd been led into. That there was nothing more beyond the wood, and there could not be. Not and also have goodness. Not and also be right.

He had wanted to believe…

He had wanted to believe that the only answer was to destroy his family.

The only answer.

Why?

This was the only time in his life he'd ever had the chance to ask someone—outside the wood—who had been there. Who knew.

Alexius might have been a young child, but he'd been there the day Lazarus had gone. He had been a witness to it.

But the words stuck in his throat. Part of him preferred the legend.

Didn't legends exist for a reason?

But he was no coward. And he knew Agnes, honest, forthright and bold, would never sit in a lie when she could be certain of the truth.

It shamed him, that he had been tempted to cloak himself in a story.

And so he spoke.

"What happened?" Lazarus asked. "The day that I disappeared?"

Alexius's face became shaded. "Our mother…

Our mother changed after that. She blamed me. As she blamed me for the loss of Dionysus. Our father too. They were never the same."

"And you?"

Alexius lowered his head, and the raw emotion Lazarus could feel coming from his brother in waves was a shock. He had not expected him to have feelings—especially not so deep—about something that had happened so long ago. "I was supposed to protect you. I was supposed to protect you and… We were children. We were children and you were lost. And I felt deeply that it was my fault, and also… That I could not have stopped it. I didn't know. But losing two brothers the way that I did, I was afraid… You know it felt like it must be my fault. It did. I was devastated to lose you," Alex said. "And I know that we can never have that time back. But in many ways I lost my family that day too. I'm so glad that you were cared for. I am. But I have missed you, Lazarus. And these things are not easy for me to talk about. I was not a man raised to feel my emotions. I couldn't. And my history with family is very complicated. I… Tinley was originally engaged to Dionysus. I was intent on seducing her away from him. The night he was killed. I have struggled with my own purity of intent for much of my life for that reason. Also for the loss of you. But Tinley has made me… She's made me different. She's made me understand things about myself that I didn't before. And she's brought me peace. Peace I didn't think I could ever have. Not a man like me. She has made me… She has made me into the King that I need to be. I hope the man as well. I wish to be a brother to you. I wish to be a brother to you in ways that I have not been. And I wish to… I wish to bring restoration to your people. The people who cared for you. You shall rule by my side."

The words were as a bullet, straight to his chest. They might have knocked him off his horse had he not found a way to steady himself.

He had not come here for this. For *restoration*.

He had not known such a thing was possible.

He had come for destruction. For in his mind the only option was conquer or be conquered.

Perhaps that was the blood of his great-grandfather. A man who had not seen how people could exist side by side.

And it shamed him.

He could see that it wasn't as simple as his brother being ignorant, or uncaring. And Lazarus himself was not more enlightened than Alexius. He simply knew different angles.

Lazarus knew some of the dark, hard things in their family history.

Alexius knew the humanity.

And if you put all of those things together, they

created a whole that was quite different than either of them had previously thought or believed.

"You would rule with me?"

"It's the only way I can see forward. We must have unity, Lazarus. We must have our family together. Life without you, life after your loss, it was dark. And there is nothing I can do about the loss of Dionysus. There is nothing I can do to put Mother and Father at peace. There is nothing I can do to change what our ancestors did to the people of the wood. I cannot go back. But we can go forward, and we can do things differently. And that is something I think we are honor bound to do."

"You do not wish for bloodshed?" Lazarus asked.

Alexius looked at him, one dark brow arched. "I do not. Were you prepared for it?"

He nodded slowly. "I was prepared for anything."

"And how does this sit with you? A truce?"

"It sits better with me than I would've thought."

He thought back to when he had nearly taken Tinley. Something to hurt his brother. Something to get revenge.

An act of open war. And he had told himself that the reasons he had given his brother for his not taking Tinley were all emotional, and he had told himself it was not true. That for him it had been about maintaining peace where he could, and giving himself time to plan things out a bit more strategically.

But the truth was, seeing the way his brother

loved Tinley had done something to him. It was something he could not understand.

"Come," Alexius said. "We will talk about logistics. And I will race you back."

And so they did. Going as fast as their horses could take them, all the way back down to the palace. And Lazarus felt something like joy. Something like freedom. Like fun. Like a childhood that had slipped through his grasp when he was four years old, never to be reclaimed. Until now. Until this moment.

And when they arrived, Tinley met them, coming out of the palace. And she was... Radiant. Her face glowed with joy as she ran toward Alexius. He dismounted his horse and picked her up from the ground, holding her gently for a kiss. And there was something... Something. Something between them that he couldn't even understand. Love, he knew that it was. But it was that same feeling he had looking at his brother from the wood when Tinley had vanished. Mystified. Furious. And it had to do with the limitations in his own soul. Even the confusion that he felt when Alexius proposed a merger. When he proposed peace. All of it was so foreign to him. Mercy. Compassion. Softness.

His mother...

He had learned to build a wall over his fear, his hurt. It was how Agamemnon had told him to survive. But he had lost so many things. So many pieces of himself.

And there was Agnes. Agnes who had wept after they'd made love. Who he held in his arms while she shook, but felt like a mountain trying to find ways to soften for a weary traveler. He did not know how. He did not know if such a thing were possible. Stone could not be made soft. And he still felt like a boy, standing in the woods, separate from this bright and brilliant world. Separate from this reality. From this truth. He was not the same as his brother. And he didn't know how to be.

Perhaps he was too shaped by those years away.

But then… Didn't the answer lie here? As to being a leader… Alexius understood softness more. Alexius understood many things he didn't, he could see it. And yes, he would have to go back to his people and say it would not be the grand coup that they had all imagined. But it would be something. And it would be better in the end.

And maybe this was the softness. Maybe it was all he had.

Tinley took hold of Alex's arm and looked up at him, the look on her face brilliant. "Did you have fun?"

"Yes," Alex said.

And Lazarus found that he would've said the same. Which was a strange realization indeed.

"Where's Agnes?"

"She's gone to the baths. We had a very nice tea, but she was tired." Tinley's eyes glowed with humor, and he could not quite say why.

"I will need to journey back into the wood tonight. I will return. But... I will need Agnes."

"Are you sure Agnes should make that journey?"

He laughed. "You forget, you have seen Agnes in quite her finest clothing. But she is the same as I am. Agnes is a warrior."

And the woman he was going to marry. It was no longer a lie. Perhaps nothing here was.

Perhaps it was... Perhaps there was a way.

"We may return tonight, but late. I will... I will see you."

By the time he found Agnes she was in their bedchamber, fully dressed.

"Put your walking clothes on," he said.

"Why?"

"We're journeying back home tonight."

"Lazarus..."

"I will explain on the way."

Lazarus was grim and silent on the journey, his disquiet nearly a physical thing. The darkness began to get oppressive, and Agnes knew that they wouldn't make it back to the encampment tonight.

"Are we to sleep out here?"

She did not fear the wolves of the wood, nor any

of the other dangers. Lazarus was the most dangerous thing in this forest.

"Sure, yes, we shall stop here."

He put their bags down, and then began the work
of making a fire. It didn't take him long before the
flames were high and hot. He was so experienced
in survival. He was just the sort of man who could
keep her safe. Who could take care of her, who
could take care of a nation.

"Do you know why we have to go back?" he
asked.

"No. Because you didn't tell me."

"And you didn't ask," he said, looking at her in-
tently.

"All right. Why?"

"I don't think… I don't think there's going to be
a revolution. I spoke to Alex, and he… He was re-
gretful to hear about the history of the country. He
wants to make it right. He wants me to rule with
him, and to represent the interests of the people of
the forest. We will talk more later about the particu-
lars, but he… He wants to restore what was taken.
He wants to find a way. For us all to coexist peace-
fully. For us to be a family."

"And that is…what you want?"

He didn't have words for what he wished. It was
a tangle of hard frustration in his chest, and he had
no idea how to say one way or the other whether
this was good or bad. Whether it was within his ex-

pectations or not. It was nothing like he had imagined. But none of this was. Lazarus had always known firmly who he was and what he was for. An instrument of vengeance if nothing else. And now... Now it was not to be so. But perhaps it was better. Perhaps this was better. But what would it mean to their people?

What would it mean to their way of life? Would they want this compromise.

"I began compromising the moment that I saw Tinley standing in that clearing. I was going to take her. I was going to make her my war bride. But then... I saw the way he went after her. I saw what he did. I do not understand those feelings. Alexius seems to have ripped himself open and carved out space for this woman inside of him and I do not understand. I can't understand. I was made to be something else entirely, and this... This road to compromise is painful like the breaking of a limb."

"Lazarus..."

"You were part of a family once. Even if you can't remember."

"So were you."

"Can you show me, Agnes? I need to understand. I need to understand why she looks at him like that when he comes back to the palace. I need to understand why he changed. That's what he told me. That Tinley changed him. That she made him see himself differently. I… I do not understand this. And I… I need to. Agnes, I need you."

Agnes felt at a loss. There was a hard edge to his voice, desperation to his words, and she did not know how she was supposed to call the answers up to these questions.

"I don't know," she said. "No one has ever cared for me, Lazarus, not really. The closest thing has been you in your obligation to me. I only know the same things you do."

"When we touch it is fire," he said. "And I can see that between them. It is that the core of what they are. At the core of their connection. Can we not find that?"

"I don't know," she said.

"Teach me," he said. "Teach me to be like him. Teach me the way to make you look at me in such a fashion."

"I don't know what you mean."

"She looks at him as if he is the sun, the moon and the stars, and I… I don't know how to be anything but the mountain."

She put her hand on his face. "The mountain has sheltered me."

"But cannot hold you," he said. "I am to be a leader to my people, and I don't know how to be a leader that is something more than blood oaths and promises of war. I have to go back there, I have to tell them. That everything has changed. I have to be different."

"Lazarus."

And then he was kissing her. And it was fierce and hard, and everything that was always between them. But there was a desperation now, a lack of control that superseded even what had occurred between them last night. Because this wasn't the snapping of self-control at the end of a seduction. It wasn't that build of desire. This was an explosion. He was angry. And he was seeking. Taking the kiss deeper and deeper, as if he could find the answers he was looking for at her very center. As if he could taste her deep enough, hold her hard enough and find what he was after.

"I want to…" But he couldn't finish the sentence. His eyes were wild, and full of black fire, and they searched hers, and she knew that she did not have the answers.

"I am no more civilized human than you."

"More fool me," he ground out. "Because I created you. In the same fashion that I was created. And it is broken. I was here deceiving my brother, with the full intent of killing him by my own hand if I had to. I would've taken his bride. I do not know compassion. I do not know mercy."

"We are showing it," she whispered. "You do know it. You rescued me from the alley…"

"With blood."

"Sometimes blood is needed. I don't know, Lazarus, maybe some people come together in glitter and fairy tales, and you and I are deadly vows and sword fights. Maybe that isn't wrong. Maybe it just is."

"Show me," he said.

His mouth was on hers again, his kisses punishing, bruising. And she gave back everything she got, trying to find the more that he was looking for, trying to call it out from inside of herself and give it to him, because he needed it so desperately, and she did not want to deny him anything she had in her that might be good. Anything that she had that he might need.

You love him.

She did. But what would he understand of those words?

He saw love between Alex and Tinley, and he could not understand it. What would the words mean if he could not understand the feeling?

"It is not fair what happened to you," she whispered against his mouth. "You were turned into a weapon, not treated as a boy."

He growled, pushing her down to the earth, his large body over the top of hers. "No talking," he said. "Show me. Show me with your body. Show me how to feel."

And that she knew she could do. That she understood. Because she had never been emotionless, however much she wanted to be. Because she had always been with him out of more than loyalty. Because she had always been with him out of love.

"Yes, my Lord."

And of her own free will she stripped the clothes from her body, bare to the soft earth, bare to him. And he stripped off his own clothing, kissing her hard and long before lifting her buttocks up off the ground and pulling her onto his body, impaling her in one swift stroke. He gripped her hips hard, guiding the movements, putting one thumb roughly between her legs and rolling it over the source of her pleasure as he continued to move her body up and down. And she let him. Let him find the rhythm that would quiet the demons in his soul. Because what he didn't realize was she didn't have to do anything. She felt. She loved him. And that was it. It made no sense. And he was right. They were two people twisted by their upbringings. And then shaped imperfectly into something that could survive.

But no one had modeled these things, these feelings for them. No one had shown them what it meant to love and be loved. And yet, she felt that way. And somehow knew that there was nothing deeper or more true than what she felt for him. Because if it wasn't love, if it wasn't the deepest, purest of loves, how could she want him in this way. Inside of her. Astride him, or him over her. How could she wish to swear her entire life to him. Possibly commit herself to an existence where she did not ever see the outside world.

You've seen the outside world.

And you've told him.

It was true. Lazarus was the first truly honorable man she had ever known. And she might've disagreed with what he was planning on doing, but she had never questioned his motivations. He was not selfish. And he was good. When given the chance to make a better choice, he was doing so. Even though it tore him to pieces. And she didn't quite know why, but she sensed that there were reasons deeper than the political.

Lazarus had never craved power. What he craved was honor and righteousness. He was a leader, through and through. And all he ever wanted to do was the right thing by his people. But there was something raw here. Something raw and wounded. And it was more than simply being raised in a Spartan environment.

Because he's afraid that no one loved him. He's afraid he doesn't know love because he's never had it.

And that was when she found her courage. That was when she whispered against his mouth, "I love you."

And he growled, pushing her down into the earth, his thrusts becoming hard and wild. And she lost her thoughts. Lost her sense of anything but this war between them. For it was always a war. A battle for pleasure. But a battle for more than that. For connection.

And perhaps that was what they were always engaged in. Whether it was a sword fight or sex. A deep need to be as close to each other as possible. To be with someone who understood. Who else understood but him? Really. And who else could understand him but her?

They had been taken from the life they had known and brought into the wood. They had lived lives where they had felt a lack of love. They had lost people who had cared for them.

And all of these things might've happened at different times, but they knew each other's feelings. Real and true.

And he might not realize that, but it was so.

"I love you," she whispered again, and then the desire inside of her boiled to overflowing. She gasped, pleasure rolling over her in a wave, and then he shuddered in her arms, kissing her as he found his own release. As he spilled himself inside of her.

And then he reached into their supplies and unrolled a large sheepskin blanket, folding it over the top of them and laying them by the fire. He said nothing. And when she awoke, the dawn was gray, and he was standing with all of their things prepared, her clothing folded next to the blanket. "We must be going," he said.

He said nothing more about what had occurred last night. And when they arrived at the village there at the center of the forest, all multilevel houses built into the sides of the hills, she waited for the lift of homecoming to bolster her spirits. But it didn't. Because there was a heaviness to Lazarus, and she could feel it echoing inside of him. And she did not think that she could feel any sort of real happiness so long as he felt this deep and terrible weight.

It was as if his own heart had been placed inside of her chest. And she could feel everything he did keenly.

"It will be well," she said.

"You don't know that," he said.

She shook her head. "No," she said. "I don't. But I know you needed to hear it." And that, she decided, would be her lesson for the day in feelings.

That sometimes you just said the thing to soothe the person you cared for because they already knew the truth, and that gesture was more important in that moment than truth could ever be.

"I'm sure the people will hear whatever you have to say."

People came out of their houses and made their way toward the main fire pit, which was roaring, early morning breakfast prepared for those who wished to eat all together. Many people ate their family meals privately, but there was always a meal prepared at the fire for anyone who might be without. For anyone who might be alone.

But they knew that Lazarus was back. They knew their King was back. And so they all came.

"I have been with my brother," he said. "King Alexius of Liri. We have decided on peace."

There was a ripple in the crowd. "Bloodshed will only bring more bloodshed. I do not want to lose any people here. Any more than my brother wants to lose his. We will be planning a way for us to have our independence. A way for me to rule alongside him. A way that will open up opportunities for everyone here, while preserving our way of life. It is about choice. Everyone here should have it."

And very much to the surprise of Lazarus and Agnes, the response was not angry. There were questions, many of them, and they passed all three meals there by the fire, talking about what would be. And when the light began to fade, people still stayed. And talked.

"I went with a single purpose. But I realized, I did not see things fully. It was only when I met my brother that I was able to see. These ideas are new, I know. But I believe *new* is the only way forward. No matter how much wisdom I could see in the old way…it will only take us back. I don't want anyone here to lose a son or daughter," Lazarus said. "A wife, a husband. A brother. That is why peace is the best path. But we shouldn't have to hide any-more. And he has promised me that isn't the case."

"It's so different from the way that Agamemnon spoke," one of the women said. "It is foreign, this thing you propose."

"Peace and mercy? I know. But I wonder if it might be the only way. The only real path. To life. It will not right every wrong. But I wonder if some-times… If sometimes there is no avenging wrongs too deeply wrought. Because what will it gain us? We will lose. In the end. We will all lose something. And for what? To satisfy a grudge that is not even ours? I will not scar us in that way."

"And if he's lying?"

"He isn't. I'm confident in that. But you have my word that my role will always be to represent our best interests."

"But you're one of them," a man said.

"I'm not," Lazarus said. "I am, and always will be, the King of the Dark Wood. This is my home. This is where I was raised. This is where I was given shelter and safety."

"A man cannot serve two masters," someone else shouted from the back.

"And I do not," he said. "I serve you. Trust me as you always have."

And all the while, Agnes stood by his side, her hand on her sword. For in the end, her loyalty was to him. And if there was a battle, she would fight for him.

In the end, they voted, they agreed. They agreed that this was the path. At least to try. And Lazarus swore to take a small band of men to the palace to be part of the discussion process.

To be part of this new world. They spoke of all the technology in education that would be open to them if they chose to take it. They spoke of opportunities. For them, for their children. Of choice.

And when they were exhausted, they went back to the palace. Lazarus's palace. The glittering, black castle deep in the rocks of the largest mountain at the back of the forest.

Spiraling turrets merged with the mountainside, all onyx and obsidian. The door was inset with gems, also made of rock, and it opened upon Lazarus's approach. The integration of technology into the wood had begun to happen before Agnes had arrived, and she was not shocked by it now. But she remembered being in awe of it at first.

Automatic doors and fingerprint sensors seemed more like magic here in this place that lacked so many of the markings of time.

It retained its medieval air while possessing a shocking amount of creature comforts within its glittering black depths.

Agnes had always found it to be home. And she

did not wait to be invited. Rather instead she followed him to his chamber.

"That went well," she said.

"Yes." There was a large tub at the back of the room, black and iron. The water came straight from the heart of the mountain spring and was heated quickly by a sophisticated system. Lazarus turned it on, and began to take his clothes off. And Agnes began to slip off her own. Without waiting to be invited. He cast a glance at her, his gaze hooded. "Would you join me?"

"I was not going to wait to be asked."

"My appreciation for you not attempting to bring a dagger into the bathtub."

"Don't give me a reason to use it and I don't feel the need to be armed."

When the tub was full, he shut the water off, stepping into it, and she followed suit, letting the hot water roll up over her skin. She pressed herself against his large body, her back against his bare chest, her bottom nestled firmly against his manhood. And they were quiet, there, in that moment. His hands comforting on her body, the warm water creating a cocoon around them. She rested her head against him. This was the first time they had been here. In this place where they had lived together for many years, not like this at all, in this changed state.

"What bothers you so much?" she asked.

He kissed her temple, and she shivered. "You, at the moment. I should like to be inside of you."

"I would like that," she said. "But that isn't what I meant."

"I know," he said. "I made my family into an enemy, Agnes, because I could not have them. Because it was easier than grief. My mother is dead. My father is dead. My youngest brother is dead. All that I will have, ever…is Alexius. And it was easier to tell myself that there could be no reconciliation. But they were… That they were everything Agamemnon said they were. Because I cannot have those years back. I cannot become the man that I would've been. I cannot… My mother used to read to me. She loved me. I know she did. I remember feeling secure. I remember feeling… Happy. I can remember playing ball with Alexius and it was fun. And when he and I rode horses yesterday, I felt that again. That's real. It has been so many long years since I felt anything like it. I was never a child here. A grim sense of duty is all I have known. And I forgot what it was to be part of the family. Having to try to remember now and realizing that those parts of myself have grown dark and weak from disuse is… I am alone," he said.

She understood. It was what he'd been chasing last night. That connection. That sense of being part of something and someone. She did understand. She understood it deeply. Because she felt the same way.

She had been with Lazarus for years, but felt like she was always holding pieces of herself back. She lived with her father, and had felt utterly outside of herself the entire time.

"Remember what I said to you about choices my father would make? About how I felt that if we were doing the same thing he would do, taking the easy way, it couldn't be right?"

"I do. It was a stinging rebuke, Agnes."

"Being who you are is not easy. Having the bravery to face these complicated things… It is not. Not in the least. This is honesty. And it forces you to be true to pieces of yourself you would rather not. I know. I understand. But isn't this better? I think this is where you might find the connection you seek."

"It hurts," he said. "Like reopening a wound to clean it."

And she did not find the analogy off-putting, because she herself was a warrior, and she understood those terms. "I know," she said. And in this moment, she felt like she might be his teacher. Much in the same way he had been hers. It made her want to laugh, but there was nothing funny about this moment. It was heavy. She felt that same heaviness that had descended upon them the moment they had come into the forest. That heaviness he was carrying with him.

"I can share your burden," she said. "I'm here. You're not alone, and neither am I. The truth is, neither of us have been, not these last eight years—it's just that you and I are so used to being an island we didn't realize when we were not."

"Do you really love me?"

He asked that question in the same tone of voice as he had said everything else during this conversation, but there was an edge to it. Just underneath the surface.

"Yes," she said. "With my heart. My body. My life. I love you."

"But you cannot mean it. Not really."

"Why not?"

"Because I am…"

And he couldn't finish that sentence either.

"I spent a great deal of time in my own thoughts, Lazarus. Trust that I know them now. That is the benefit of this kind of lonely life."

"And yet I feel as if I know nothing."

"Good for you," she said. "You're otherwise always so certain. Perhaps a bit of uncertainty will do you well." Then he lifted her up from the tub, kissing her, but different than he had done by the fire. This was gentle.

This was something she didn't know. A tender touch, his rough palms skimming her bare skin as he brought her down onto the bed. Both of them were still wet, but she didn't mind, and he didn't seem to either. His kisses were sweet, but not in the way they had been that night he had been attempting a seduction. This was an attempt at nothing. It simply was.

And she knew they were both mindless. Desperate with need for each other. Desperate for things that only the other could provide.

He kissed every inch of her skin, and she felt right, incandescent with her need for him. Then he positioned himself over her, entered her slowly. This coupling didn't have the wildness of last night, didn't have the violence of their first time. Didn't have the calculation of their first kisses. This was simply Lazarus and Agnes. As they were, as they might've been. As everything. And in that moment, she had to wonder if each sharp and broken rock on the paths that they had walked had been left there for this specific purpose.

And she felt nearly ashamed. To think that perhaps his fate had never been what he had imagined, and that her fate had never been simply to swear loyalty to him. But that their fate was now. In this slow, deep build of intimacy that was teaching her things with each and every stroke of his hardness inside of her. It was more than pleasure. More than simple connection. This wasn't the blind fumbling of two people simply in the throes of lust. They touched here at their souls. This was stripping layers off them both. Layers of protectiveness. Layers of damage done by the world. Done by the people who were supposed to care for them. Or in Lazarus's case, by the loss of the people who had loved him very much.

This was something real.

She began to tremble with pleasure, and she felt an answering quiver in his muscles. And when he found his release, she found hers at the same moment, and he cradled her face, pressing his forehead against hers, growling with the intensity of it. And her cries mingled with his, echoing off of the stone walls. And she knew that this was always meant to be. These walls were always meant to house their mixed cries of release. And she snuggled against him, beneath the covers. Her hand on his chest.

"We go back to Liri in the morning," he said. "We will try to make the journey in one day. Are you prepared for that?"

"Yes," she said.

"I should not have dragged you here."

"You need me," she said.

And she looked up at him. "It's okay to admit that."

"I need you," he said.

A rush of relief washed over her. For it was all she had wanted to hear from him. All she had wanted to hear from him that night in Paris when she had ambushed him with the sword. And she had been told that he did not. She needed him. It was only fair that he needed her right back.

"Good. Then there should be no more talk of sending me away."

CHAPTER TWELVE

THE ENTIRE JOURNEY back to the palace, Lazarus felt a strange sort of frustration. He wanted to do something for Agnes. And he did not know what. He wanted to give her something. In truth, he wanted to give her everything, but he certainly didn't know how to accomplish that. And he had to focus on the task at hand. Joining these two people together, working out the details of it with his brother and figuring out how a joint leadership situation worked. He did not need to be obsessing about a woman who had been his shield maiden up until a couple of weeks ago.

Still, they stopped and took a break, and Agnes seemed like she was filled with some sort of forest magic as she hopped from rock to rock, until she was up at the top of a very tall one, sitting with one knee pulled up and the other leg dangling over the edge of the moss-covered stone. She looked like a fairy. And she was to be his fairy princess, he supposed.

While Agnes sat and drank in the rays of the sun, he went into a thicket and found vines and flowers. He had learned to make things out of vines very early, a practical technique when you lived in a place with so many. He quickly fashioned together a crown, placing flowers all around, feeling especially silly as his large hands moved over the delicate material. And when Agnes came down, he placed it upon her head. "If I am to be a King," he said.

Her dark eyes shone bright, and she smiled, bigger than any of the smiles she had given when he had brought her designer dresses. No, she had looked more annoyed about those than anything else. But this… This thing fashioned from the forest she was alight with joy over.

It did something to ease the knowing feeling in his chest, but not everything because he still felt…

Agnes had lived such a difficult life. Didn't she deserve a man who had not? He had asked her to show him what feeling looked like, he had desperately begged her to, and based on what?

He knew full well that what he was asking of Agnes was… It was unfair. Asking her to fix these things inside of him when he had no reasonable method of fixing anything in her. Nor did he have any expectation of being able to do so. It was not fair.

And yet, when he looked at her, with her crown of flowers on her face full of sunshine, he could do nothing but continue to walk with her. For he was losing his grip on all that he was supposed to be, and Agnes felt like an anchor. She felt like the path forward. Like the thing that might make all of this possible.

Things had gone well in the wood. And not only that, she felt the bond between herself and Lazarus grow stronger.

It was not about things that they owed each other, not anymore. And now that he was firmly set on joining forces with his brother, she could breathe. She didn't have that horrible knot in her chest when she looked at Tinley. In fact, she and Tinley were becoming friends, and it was a wonderful thing. Agnes could not remember the last time she had a friend. She wasn't sure she ever really had. Growing up, she had moved around so often, and she had never wanted to lie to the girls that she had come into contact with, as usually, her father was swindling their parents. Consequently, she had been very lonely. Always. And she loved Lazarus, with all of her heart. Her days with him here at the palace were not as intense as the time they'd once spent together. He had other duties. He was currently entrenched in meetings with Alexius, and the other men of the wood, trying to figure out a reasonable system of government. Trying to figure out how to… Rewrite a nation. It wasn't easy. But they were good men, and they were doing their best, and whatever they didn't get perfectly, Agnes had absolute certainty they would sort out when the problems were identified.

The nights though… They were a great deal more intense than the nights they had spent together before.

He took her in his arms every night at bedtime, and turned to her multiple times between fits of sleep. He was insatiable, and so was she. Reaching for that connection they had found with each other, and only each other. And she knew it to be true. With him as well as with her.

That he felt exactly the same thing she did. It was a glorious thing, this.

They had spoken no more about marriage, though, and she realized that she had never formally accepted him. She had simply… Not refused him. And she found that she wanted him to ask again. Even if that was silly. And after they had been at the palace for two weeks, it filtered down to Tinley that Lazarus was planning something.

"All I know is he has asked for there to be many cakes," Tinley said, grinning.

"Then it is certainly for me," Agnes said, feeling jittery.

"Do you care to tell me the whole story of your relationship with Lazarus?"

There was no reason not to tell Tinley, not now.

"Well," Agnes said. "It is just that we were not engaged when we came. He was… He thought that it would soften his image. If he pretended that we were in love."

"I see," Tinley said. "But you… You were in love with him."

Agnes nodded. "I am. I have been. That much was true. I have been in love with him since I was sixteen. I love him with all that I am. And now, as things have changed between us I can only hope that he loves me too. But I don't know. I don't know, and I don't know that I shall. I don't know that he'll ever speak of his feelings. It's okay. He has said that he wants to marry me. In truth."

Tinley nodded slowly. "I know a whole lot about men who have difficulties opening up their hearts. The Alexius that you have met is very different than the one that I knew for most of my life. He was a stone wall. And I was so convinced that I loved his brother that I could not understand the overwhelming feelings that took me over completely when I was in his presence. He was and is the best of men, though. And it was true even before he could figure out how to tell me what he felt. Things between us were not easy. Not in the beginning. Not when he was… Not when he was trying to figure everything out. That was very difficult for him. As I mentioned before, he was so scarred by the loss of Lazarus, by the loss of Dionysus…"

"I fear that Lazarus has begun to address his scars," Agnes said.

"So the question is, what are you willing to do for him? Do you require that he be able to tell you he loves you? Do you require that he be able to show it in exactly the same way you show him?"

She thought back to when she had been a girl, taken in from the streets of Paris. She thought back to how he had rescued her. And taught her to fight, slowly and painstakingly. How her muscles had been soft at first before becoming honed, her instincts finely tuned. You were what you were made. But you could become something different. But it did not happen overnight. And it took someone who was willing to come alongside you and help with the reshaping. He had done it for her. Could she do any less for him?

"I am willing to meet him where he is. Because whether it's tomorrow or thirty years, when he finally says the words, when he's finally able to… I will feel the same. Whether I'm here or somewhere else. Whether I am off in Paris pretending to laugh while I drink champagne, or sitting in the palace and the wood with him. And I would rather be with him."

"I knew the moment I met you that you were as good a woman as there was, Agnes. The exact woman strong enough to love my brother-in-law. I have known the two of you for the exact same amount of time. But I see so much of Alexius in him. And I feel a great deal for him based on Alexius's feelings. You are exactly what he needs."

Agnes nodded, but then Tinley continued, "Is he able to be what you need?"

"Did you care? When you were having to decide about Alexius?"

Tinley offered her a rueful smile, and then shook her head. "No. I confess I didn't much care as long as I was with him."

"It is the same for me. There are many things out there in the world, and my father spent his entire life chasing them. Fortune, esteem. He was always after something that he could not grasp. And he had a child right beside him who would've loved him, if only he would have spared one single moment to look my way. But he saw me only as a tool, and nothing more. He saw me as something to be used. I have been out in the world. I have been to most countries in Europe. I have learned languages. I have been rich off of the money of other people, and very poor. But never have I been happier than when I was by Lazarus's side. No matter the nature of our relationship. It is the people in our lives that make it worth living. Circumstances change. But if you can never look to who is beside you, who would stay beside you no matter what, then you will never truly find happiness. My father died unhappy, in front of his child, who only ever wanted his love."

"You are young, Agnes," Tinley said. "But your soul isn't."

"I don't think Lazarus or I ever had the luxury of young souls."

"I hope tonight brings you what you want."

Lazarus was planning on proposing to her. Really proposing to her. He had visions of her as his bride, a crown of flowers in her hair, like the one he had made her in the wood. Yes, he could adorn her in gold, and might even like to sometimes, but mostly, he wanted her as his forest fairy. His little earthen warrior. For anyone could gleam in gold, but it took someone truly special to glow with vines and leaves.

And his Agnes was special.

Alexius had suggested a picnic on the lawn, as it was a gesture he had used with Tinley, and one that she had liked very much. Lazarus didn't quite know what to do with this new brotherly relationship. This new input that he received from him. It was a strange thing indeed. And yet, he could not say he was opposed to it.

When she came out onto the balcony, his heart caught in his chest. She was wearing a bright orange dress he had not seen before. The fabric flowed over her curves like liquid. The deep gold of her skin made the color catch fire, and her hair, glossy and dark, was arranged in a beautiful style high on her head. There were little orange flowers placed throughout, and she was exactly as he had just been thinking. A forest fairy.

A forest fairy who could cut him.

His body responded with intense pleasure.

He cared for this woman. Would fight armies to ensure her safety. She smiled when she saw him, and that was when he noticed she had gold makeup on her cheeks, her eyes.

"Did Tinley have a hand in this?"

She blushed.

"Yes. Do you like it?"

He wrapped his arms around her waist. And he kissed her, with all of the hunger inside of him. "It is a good thing we are in a semipublic space."

"Is it?" she asked, lifting a brow.

It was strange how they could know each other as they did, and still find new ways to speak. New ways to be. Their relationship had been marked by seriousness for a great number of years, but now they could laugh. And he could touch her. However he wished. And she seemed to enjoy it. She also returned the favor, with frequency.

That was one thing he liked very much about Agnes. She returned his enthusiasm for making love with passion and intensity. Gave as good as she got.

His physical equal in all things, as he had suspected.

She walked out to the center of the lawn, where

there was a table and chairs set out for them, lights strung overhead.

"It's beautiful." She looked toward the wood, a strange smile touching her lips. "Isn't it odd, how it feels like were in an entirely different world and we're only about two hundred feet away from where we came from?"

She looked abashed. "Well, I guess you started out here."

His chest went tight of a sudden. Because of course he had come from here. It had been this very lawn where they had been playing before he had wandered into the woods.

"I know what you mean," he said.

"Good," she said.

He looked at her as she sat at the table, with the wood behind her. And he realized… It was so. He had not really gone anywhere. And neither had she.

Hadn't he promised her something more? Hadn't he promised her experiences?

And he supposed it was only a man with a very big ego who would consider his body the experience that she required.

And no one could ever accuse him of having a small ego, it was true. But that was not all he wanted for her.

And there was something… There was something stifling about sitting here like this. On the lawn. He should've thought more critically about this. Should've thought more deeply about how it would feel to sit here with her.

But he had told her he wanted to marry her, and it was true.

It was true. In his pocket, he had a ring. Alexius had brought in tray upon tray from a jeweler down in Liri's largest city. And he had selected the grandest for Agnes.

He knew that it was something a lot more ostentatious than her typical style, but it had to do with what he wanted to give her. Which was simply everything.

Everything he could. And it was in his pocket now. Ready for him to propose to her, because he felt that she deserved that at least. Not these demands that he had been making of her before.

And yet, all of this was beginning to get tangled up. In the promise he made to her before. How had things changed?

And she had declared that she wanted to be free, had she not?

But then, he had dismissed that as injured pride, since she had clearly been furious with him when he'd said he didn't need her.

And the fact was, he did need her. He needed her more than he could ever say. He needed her in a deep, profound sense, and there was a strange twisting and burning in his chest, and suddenly, Agnes rose from her seat.

"It's funny, this, how it hit everybody for so long, how these woods tore so many lives apart out here, but you and I simply saw home."

Had he? Had he really seen it as his home?

"Have a seat," he said. "Dinner will be coming soon."

And of course, he wasn't afraid of the wood. But for some reason he didn't like the image of her standing there at the edge of it. He could remember when he had been the dangerous thing lying in the deep waiting for Tinley. He didn't like… He didn't like seeing Agnes in that position. And it clotted another memory too. One that he simply didn't want to have.

"It's funny," she said. "How we never see the wolves."

"They're real," he said. "I've seen them."

"Yes. I just mean… I was only commenting that it's funny how…"

"Yes," he said, a leaden weight in his stomach.

Their meal came, and he did his best to brush off the strange feelings coursing through him. There was steak and bread, cursory vegetables, though he knew that Agnes didn't really want them. And afterward, trays of cakes, which he knew for certain she did want.

They ate, and all the while, he was planning on issuing his proposal as soon as they were through.

But then they finished, and Agnes got up from her chair again, wandering to the edge of the wood.

He could follow her. Ask her.

He stood from the chair, and overwhelmingly, abruptly, the images in front of him were not the images of now. He began to have flashes of memory. His ball, bouncing to the edge of the wood. And he stopped, looking inside. And he could see something. Something moving. And then he saw a hand scoop the ball and take it farther into the trees. He remembered being afraid. But he was a prince. There was nothing he should be afraid of, not in his kingdom. He and his brother played with wooden swords, and they were heroes. He knew exactly what to do if there was a foe. Prince Lazarus did not run. And he wanted his ball.

So he went forward into the darkness. And that was when he realized his first mistake. It was impossible to see. But then he could see his ball, somewhere deeper, and in he went. And just for one moment, he saw a man's face, hiding in the bushes, right behind the ball.

Agamemnon.

Agamemnon.

It had not been an accident that he had been in the woods. He had been lured there.

It had been the plan. All along.

The wolves…

There were wolves. But Agnes was right. Why did they hear from them not at all now? And why…

A sour feeling turned in the pit of his stomach. *Dogs.*

The dogs that Lazarus had cared for, until the pack had eventually reached old age and died. The same dogs that had torn his face to shreds.

At the behest of their master.

Agamemnon was the one who wanted to stage a bloody rebellion, and he had been intent on using Lazarus to do so. He had also not intended to die, Lazarus was certain of that. But he had.

Everything… Everything had been a lie. He hadn't been saved. He had been brought in and manipulated. Trained. He knew that what Agamemnon had told him about the land being stolen from their people was true. He had done his research outside of Liri. Agamemnon's anger had come from a real place, but what he had done…

And he must be responsible for the death of Lazarus's brother, the one he had never met. Of Dionysus. For it could only be Agamemnon's dogs. Of course. This idea that the wolves never touch those who lived in the wood… They were kept contained. And he had listened to folk tales and fairy stories and taken them on as real because he had been wounded that his family had not come for him.

And he had nearly… He would've killed his own brother in the name of Agamemnon's vengeance, a bloody vengeance that would serve no one. Because he had been the only father he'd ever known and remembered and he would have…

He'd have done anything for him.

Nearly had.

His family was not cursed. They were targeted. And those things were not the same.

Targeted for the sins of a great-grandfather that they had never met. Something they had never known about.

Their entire life had been twisted, his own uprooted.

He didn't know anything about himself. And the raw horror that was bleeding through his chest made it impossible for him to think. He was nothing that he thought he was. Nothing. And here he was, trying to bind Agnes to him, and for what? As a Band-Aid to all the shortcomings inside of his own soul? It could not be endured. Not for Agnes.

He could not do this to her. The anger that was inside of his veins was a crushing, suffocating thing. And it would destroy him. It would destroy her along with it.

He wanted… He had been desperate for her. Desperate for her to teach him to love. Desperate to feel some kind of connection with another human, and he did. But he didn't know how to give it back. His veins were full of poison. He had spent his life being conned. And he hated it. He hated all of this.

He could not in good conscience keep her with him. Everything he was, was a lie. And everything he had believed in…

He had believed that Agamemnon had saved his life, that he must follow this arcane practice of being bound to him because of that. He had thought that Agamemnon had taught him all those things out of care, but it had never been that. The only father figure that he could remember had simply been manipulating him. Using him. He had not gotten lost in the wood; he had been stolen from the palace. His life had not been saved; he had been put in danger by the very man who professed to rescue him.

And from that had come Agnes. And his bonding her to him. And she was so grateful. The same way that he was to Agamemnon.

How could he ask her to form any feelings for him based on that?

All of it was a sick life. All of it.

How could he propose to her now? How could he promise her anything?

The simple truth was he could not.

He had to let her go. He had to tell her to leave.

To go to Paris or back to Ohio or wherever she wanted to be. He had to set her free. Because her feelings were born from an arcane practice that put too much weight on the person who was saved.

She had to have a chance. The chance he had never been given. To unlearn what he had been taught. To decide what manner of person he was for himself.

He could not use Agnes as a surrogate for a heart that he had never been able to develop because of the way that he had been shaped.

It was not fair.

For inside of him was anger, and it was nothing like the connection between Alexius and Tinley. Nothing at all.

Nothing at all.

And when he did not propose, he could see the disappointment on her face. But she didn't know.

He was standing there going over the scorched, destroyed remains of his soul. And she didn't know.

They went back to their room, and she began to undress. He stopped her. "Agnes, there is something I must say."

She turned to face him, her expression full of hope. And it was his job to kill it, and she would not understand that it was a mercy. But he had to separate her from him. He owed her that. He could not keep her under the weight of this terrible responsibility.

"Agnes, I am going to get you an apartment. Wherever you would like. Anywhere in the entire world. And have you enroll at a university there."

"What?"

"We talked about this. That you wished to be free."

"That was before," she said. "Surely you must realize that was before."

"No. It must be now. It was easy for me to keep you. Because you would make a lovely Queen for me, and you must know that. You are beautiful. And you are strong. And as I said to you… The only woman that has ever been able to withstand all that I wish to give her. And giving that up is a very difficult thing."

"Is that all?"

He nodded slowly, the lie pushing against the back of his throat. "That is all. I realized some things, and I…"

"What?"

"What I wanted from you, what I demanded of you with the fire that night… I don't understand love, Agnes. I am what I was made."

"Agamemnon cared for you…"

"Agamemnon lied to me," he said. "I did not realize it until… Until we were standing there at the edge of the wood. And then I remembered. I remembered that he was there. I remembered that he lured me there to the wood. Yes, I remembered. And once I remembered… I realize that none of it was true. None of it. Down to you being bonded to me. Because it is a chain. A chain of lies, is it not? He stole me from my family. And he told me they didn't care about me. And that was the man that I was raised by. No one loved me, Agnes."

"I do," she said.

"Because you were bound to me. And I know what that does to you. I know. Because it was what I had. It was what I had with him and…"

"It is not the same," Agnes said. "If you really think I'm strong, if you really think that I know my mind, then how can you dismiss me like this?"

"I do it for your own good," he growled.

"You do it for yours," Agnes said. "Don't you think that I see the fear in you?"

Her words were like a sword. Pointed, as they were in reality. "This has frightened you. And I know you're sending me away because I frighten you too."

"No," he said.

"It is grief, Lazarus. It's grief that you're feeling. Because whether or not he deserved that, you did care for him. You did. And it causes you pain that he lied to you. That is normal."

"No," he said. "It isn't so simple."

"Then tell me. Explain it to me so that I can understand. It might not be simple, but neither am I," Agnes said. "I can understand you. Maybe better than you realize."

"Nobody…"

"No one can understand you? Have you ever tried? Who knows you, Lazarus? Who knows you apart from me? Don't tell me that I can't understand. I am probably the person who can understand you

the most. The best. Because we've talked. We have
spent time together. And I care about you. I care
about you beyond your connection to the royal family, beyond these missions. I care about you. So tell
me. Tell me what frightens you, and I will… I will
pick up my sword."

"I'm not frightened of anything. I'm simply fac-
ing the reality of what is. If Agamemnon lied to me,
he did not save me. If he did not save me, we were
never bonded. And you deserve the chance to find
out who you are for yourself."

"I know. I already know. Lazarus, I have played
a great many parts in my life. At the behest of my
father. I have done what he has asked me to. I know
when I'm longing. I know when I'm being lied to.
This, what we have, what I feel, it's real. It's real
and I know it. You do not need to teach me. Not in
this. Perhaps I need to teach you."

"No. That is not your job. You do not…"

"Stop telling me how strong you think I'm not.
If you have one downfall with me, that is it. I am
not the girl you found in that alley." And then suddenly, she stopped. "Maybe I am. Maybe I am the
girl that you found in that alley. And I was stronger
then too. Because I survived. I survived that day,
and yes I had you. But I had survived every day up
until that point. And I may not have done so with a
sword, but I did survive. And you keep telling me
you don't need me. You keep telling me that you

can fight without me. But what if you can't. What if I am a strength you didn't know you had. What if I am more than your shield maiden. What if I'm your heart?"

"You must go," he said. "There can be no discussion. I am not cutting you out of my life, Agnes. I am going to continue to take care of you…"

"I would love to tell you no. I would love to not accept. But the fact of the matter is, I cannot afford that. I cannot afford to live without your protection. And those things are physical, so I can't deny them. I must have shelter. I must be able to learn a trade if I'm to be on my own. So I must take what you have offered. Maybe you need me in ways that you cannot see."

He turned away from her, his heart a slow, dull thud in his ears. "I will have you sent wherever you wish."

"So that's it? I don't get to choose?"

"You get to choose. Wherever you wish to go."

"Paris then," she said. "Send me to Paris."

With a wave of his hand he dismissed her. "It is done."

CHAPTER THIRTEEN

IT HAD BEEN a week since he had sent Agnes away. A week since he had seen her. A week since he had held her in his arms.

For good reason.

He had hardly been able to sort through that dread that had filled his chest when he'd realized the truth of his background. Since then he had spoken to Alexius about it at length. But they had not talked at all of Agnes.

Tinley had taken to giving him long looks that spoke of her deep disapproval. But he could not please Tinley. In truth, he could not please himself. It was possible he could not please anyone.

He was okay with that. Everyone else would have to learn to be.

It wasn't until dinner on the night that marked exactly a week since Agnes left, that his brother finally addressed the situation.

"And is Agnes returning to us?"

"No," he said.

He had set her up with a lovely apartment in Paris, and had hired someone to guide her in enrollment in a university there. Last he heard she had not chosen what she was to study. But then, she was angry at him, so it was entirely possible she wasn't telling anyone what she was thinking because she didn't want it to filter back to him. But she... She loved him. And there was nothing he could do with that.

"I see. And why is that?"

"Agnes needs to go and experience life on her own. There are things about our relationship that you don't know..."

"Not true," Tinley said. "I told him everything Agnes told me. We have no secrets, my husband and I."

"Great," he said, his tone dry.

"I have told you what I learned about my past. That I was taken. Our family is not cursed. We were targeted. It is a very different thing. And I..."

The words that had been about to come out of his mouth were foreign to his mind. He had not ever thought them before. And he hadn't known he was about to speak them.

"The one person that I spent my life trusting lied to me," he said. "Not about what happened in our history. But about the part that I was to play.

He had already set about exacting revenge on our family. He is the reason that Dionysus was killed."

"I know," Alexius said, his voice rough. "And I know that this may make no sense to you, but there is something of a comfort in that for me, because I was sure that... That it was something in me. Something that I had done."

"Aren't you both a pair," Tinley said. "Look at you. Sitting there and comparing the darkness inside of you. It wasn't your fault," she said. "Any more than it's yours." She directed the last part to Lazarus. "It isn't your fault, and Agnes knows that. Agnes loves you."

"That isn't it," he said. "I don't blame myself for the things that were set in motion before I was born. But what I do blame myself for is... I trusted the wrong person. How can I ever trust anything inside of myself ever again?"

And that was the truth of it. How could he ever trust his heart? How could he ever trust his feelings? Agnes said that she loved him, and he was... There was something in him that was desperate for that. That clawed rapidly at his chest, wanting to get free. Wanting to touch her. Wanting to be near her, to be consumed by it. But his feelings were not trustworthy. They told lies. And what could that mean for her? He did not worry about his own pain.

Do you not?

He thought of Agnes, beautiful and bright. And

he thought of how he had sent her away. On his request. At his choice. In his timing. What if she decided to leave one day? What if he began to believe that love between them, and it turned out that it was not so? It was simply her own inexperience. It was simply…

"There are many people in this world who lie," Tinley said. "My own mother long acted as if there was something irrevocably broken in me. I understand what it is to not be certain of your place in the world because of what the people around you have said. But when someone comes along who says they love you, who has shown you they love you… Has she not shown you, Lazarus? Has she not been there for you? Agnes has been loyal and brave and true. It is more than words. It's more than feelings. It's eight years of action. She loves you."

"But…"

"And you're afraid. You're afraid of that pain you felt when you lost your family. But ask yourself this, do you feel any better now?"

He looked at his soon-to-be sister-in-law. "I don't know what I feel. I don't know how to feel anything beyond… I fear I don't understand love."

"If Agnes's life were in danger, would you risk yours to help her?"

"Every time," he said.

"If she was cold and she needed something to

keep warm, would you take the cloak off your back for her?"

"I would," he said.

"If another woman wanted to share your bed, but you knew that it would hurt her…"

"I want no one else."

"What do you think love is?"

"I've seen the two of you together. There is a softness there, a sweetness that I cannot understand."

"We've grown into that," Alex said.

"It's true," Tinley said. "At first it was all very frightening. Very painful and sharp. And sometimes the sharpness is still there. But we have grown to trust in this love. And at first it's hard to do that. Love is not comfortable when it's breaking through the barriers that you've put up around your heart. In fact, then love can be very, very painful."

Well, he had the pain.

"But what do you do? How do you guarantee that everything will be okay?"

"You can't," Alex said. "It's impossible to guarantee that anything will be okay. The Dark Wood is still there, and there are still monsters. That is the way of the world. But being in love, having someone to walk alongside you, it makes it not half so terrifying. When you can find the person who makes the sharp things worth it, then you hang on to them."

"You may not trust your own heart, Lazarus," Alex said slowly. "But do you trust Agnes?"

Agnes. Who was everything bright and brilliant and good. How could he not trust her? It was fear causing him to hide like this. Fear and he knew it. And as Agnes had said before she had gone, a deep underestimating of her strength. Which was simply not fair. Not when she had done nothing but swear loyalty to him. Unending and true.

And then love.

And what had he sworn to her? Nothing. If he felt like he wasn't known, it was because he had never let his guard down.

And what was it that Alex had said? That love, when breaking through those walls, was nothing but extremely painful. He believed it. He believed it because he felt it. It was not her. It was not her that lacked strength.

It was him. Because there was more to strength than being hard. More to strength than being a mountain. It was the softness, the vulnerability that Agnes possessed, that was where the real strength lay.

Hadn't she said just that? What if she was his heart?

What if she was his heart.

And he had torn his heart out, had torn his heart out and sent it to Paris. And for what? To try to keep himself safe. Safe from more pain. Safe from betrayal. For hadn't it been that betrayal that had caused him to change course?

That... That slap in the face of realizing that he'd been wrong.

Are you so weak? She stood there and said she accepted you regardless. She always has. And you turned away because of fear.

"And what if I went to get her?" Lazarus asked.

"Go," Tinley said, at the same time as Alexius said, "You should."

"I want to get to her as quickly as possible."

"I have a private jet," Alexius said. "You should take that."

"I won't argue."

CHAPTER FOURTEEN

AGNES WAS ALL out of tears. That was what she told herself, every day when she got up in the morning and pored over the catalog for the university she was supposed to start soon. Every afternoon when she went for a walk around the park and then the museums. Every evening when she went and got some bread or crepes and sat by the Eiffel Tower as she had done when she'd been sixteen.

Then she got into bed at night and wept again.

Because she wasn't out of tears for Lazarus. She feared she never would be. Behold, she was Agnes, unto herself. Free and unable to be anything more than a puddle of tears.

She sat in front of the tower and pulled a chunk of bread from a wax paper bag and stared straight ahead. At least she had bread now, and weeping to look forward to later.

Then, down in front of her, she saw a pair of black, shiny shoes. And there was no reason at all that shiny black shoes should trigger anything in her, except everything went still.

Then she looked up. And up yet still.

And it was him.

Lazarus.

Here.

In Paris.

At the tower.

"A girl once told me," he said, coming to sit on the cement curb beside her, "that she came here and dreamed of finding someone to love her."

Agnes's heart was beating hard in her head. "Did she? A foolish girl."

"I'm sorry to hear that," he said. "Because I had hoped to sit here. And dream awhile."

Her heart twisted painfully. "You don't need to dream. You had someone who loved you."

He sighed, the sound heavy. Deep and from his soul, and not part of this game he was playing at all. "I was afraid of that." He looked at her. "Agnes, I am so sorry. I was afraid. As you accused me of being, I was a coward. I thought…the grief that I feel over realizing I put my trust in the wrong person is… I wasn't prepared for that. My life is a lie and in that moment I decided everything must be, but Agnes, that was me being foolish. You have never been a lie. You have always been all that is true and just and faithful. And you showed me in a hundred ways what love was, what loyalty was.

And I… Everything in my chest was this great and terrible sharpness and I thought that could not be love. But a wise man told me that love is very painful when it is knocking down the walls you've built around your heart."

"Oh… Lazarus." Tears pushed against her eyes. "It is that."

"I am here, even if I am late. I am here in Paris to say that I love you. That whatever the truth about Agamemnon, my path led me to you. And that was not a mistake. It was not a lie. We are true. This is true."

She threw her arms around his neck and started to weep, and he held her. This softness, this closeness, so different to where they had started. And so deeply, wonderfully true.

"I want you to marry me. Not for show. Not because I need a wife." They parted and he wiped the tears from her cheeks. "Because I need you."

And in that moment she thought about the past, the present and the future all at once, and feared none of it.

She was that girl that had sat here and dreamed. She was the woman in his arms, now and forever.

Then he took her hand and drew her up so they were standing.

And he turned and began to walk away.

"Where are you going?"

He paused and looked at her. "We are going home."

She laughed, the echo of that first day they'd met, when he'd saved her life, clear. "And where is that?"

He took two steps back to her, then cupped her chin in his hands. "For me? Home is wherever you are. It can be here while you do school, or back in Liri. Either way, all will be well. I trust Alexius."

"You would let me stay here?"

"If you wanted."

She laughed. "You know, I think we should go back to the Dark Wood."

"You just like the bathtub."

"That is true."

He leaned in and kissed her mouth. "Wherever we go, Agnes of My Heart, one thing is true. You have saved my life. And I swear my fealty to you. For all of my days."

* * * * *

If you were captivated by
A Bride for the Lost King
why not read the first installment in
The Heirs of Liri duet?
His Majesty's Forbidden Temptation

And don't forget to check out these other
Maisey Yates stories!

The Spaniard's Stolen Bride
His Forbidden Pregnant Princess
The Queen's Baby Scandal
Crowning His Convenient Princess
Crowned for My Royal Baby

Available now!

#3937 CINDERELLA'S DESERT BABY BOMBSHELL
Heirs for Royal Brothers
by Lynne Graham

Penniless Tatiana Hamilton must marry Prince Saif after his original bride, her cousin, disappears. The ice-cold sheikh promises to end their sham marriage quickly. Until their chemistry grows too hot to ignore...and Tati discovers she's pregnant!

#3938 A CONSEQUENCE MADE IN GREECE
by Annie West

Cora thinks she knows Strato's rich, privileged type. But the man she uncovers during their no-strings encounters is captivating. A man whose past made him swear never to marry or become a father—and whose baby she's now carrying...

#3939 NINE MONTHS TO TAME THE TYCOON
Innocent Summer Brides
by Chantelle Shaw

Their blazing chemistry was more than enough to tempt Lissa into her first night of sensual abandon with Takis. Now she's pregnant... and he's demanding they turn one night into marriage vows!

#3940 THE SICILIAN'S FORGOTTEN WIFE
by Caitlin Crews

Innocent Josselyn agreed to marry dangerously compelling Cenzo, unaware of his desire for revenge against her family. But when an accident causes him to forget everything—except their electrifying chemistry—the tables are turned...

HPCNMRA0821

#3941 THE WEDDING NIGHT THEY NEVER HAD
by Jackie Ashenden

As king, Cassius requires a real queen by his side. Not Inara, his wife in name only. But when their unfulfilled desire finally gives her the courage to ask for a true marriage, can Inara be the queen he needs?

#3942 MANHATTAN'S MOST SCANDALOUS REUNION
The Secret Sisters
by Dani Collins

When the paparazzi mistake Nina for a supermodel, she takes refuge in her ex's New York penthouse. Big mistake. She's reminded of just how intensely seductive Reve can be. And how difficult it will be to walk away...again.

#3943 BEAUTY IN THE BILLIONAIRE'S BED
by Louise Fuller

Guarded billionaire Arlo Milburn never expected to find gorgeous stranger Frankie Fox in his bed! While they're stranded on his private island, their intense attraction brings them together... But can it break down his walls entirely?

#3944 THE ONLY KING TO CLAIM HER
The Kings of California
by Millie Adams

Innocent queen Annick knows there are those out there looking to destroy her. Turning to dark-hearted Maximus King is the answer, but she's shocked when he proposes a much more permanent solution—marriage!

YOU CAN FIND MORE INFORMATION ON UPCOMING HARLEQUIN TITLES, FREE EXCERPTS AND MORE AT HARLEQUIN.COM.

HPCNMRB0821

Get 4 FREE REWARDS!

We'll send you 2 FREE Books plus 2 FREE Mystery Gifts.

Harlequin Presents books feature the glamorous lives of royals and billionaires in a world of exotic locations, where passion knows no bounds.

FREE Value Over $20

YES! Please send me 2 FREE Harlequin Presents novels and my 2 FREE gifts (gifts are worth about $10 retail). After receiving them, if I don't wish to receive any more books, I can return the shipping statement marked "cancel." If I don't cancel, I will receive 6 brand-new novels every month and be billed just $4.55 each for the regular-print edition or $5.80 each for the larger-print edition in the U.S., or $5.49 each for the regular-print edition or $5.99 each for the larger-print edition in Canada. That's a savings of at least 11% off the cover price! It's quite a bargain! Shipping and handling is just 50¢ per book in the U.S. and $1.25 per book in Canada.* I understand that accepting the 2 free books and gifts places me under no obligation to buy anything. I can always return a shipment and cancel at any time. The free books and gifts are mine to keep no matter what I decide.

Choose one: ☐ **Harlequin Presents**
Regular-Print
(106/306 HDN GNWY)

☐ **Harlequin Presents**
Larger-Print
(176/376 HDN GNWY)

Name (please print)

Address   Apt. #

City   State/Province   Zip/Postal Code

Email: Please check this box ☐ if you would like to receive newsletters and promotional emails from Harlequin Enterprises ULC and its affiliates. You can unsubscribe anytime.

Mail to the **Harlequin Reader Service:**
IN U.S.A.: P.O. Box 1341, Buffalo, NY 14240-8531
IN CANADA: P.O. Box 603, Fort Erie, Ontario L2A 5X3

Want to try 2 free books from another series? Call 1-800-873-8635 or visit www.ReaderService.com.

HP21R

SPECIAL EXCERPT FROM

⊕ HARLEQUIN

PRESENTS

*Innocent Josselyn agreed to marry dangerously
compelling Cenzo, unaware of his desire for revenge
against her family. But when an accident causes him to
forget everything—except their electrifying chemistry—
the tables are turned...*

*Read on for a sneak preview of
Caitlin Crews's next story for Harlequin Presents,*
The Sicilian's Forgotten Wife.

"I wish only to kiss my wife," Cenzo growled. "On this, the first
day of the rest of our life together."

"You don't want to kiss me." She threw the words at him, and
he thought the way she trembled now was her temper taking hold.
"You want to start what you think will be my downward spiral,
until all I can do is fling myself prostrate before you and cringe
about at your feet. Guess what? I would rather die."

"Let us test that theory," he suggested and kissed her.

And this time, it had nothing at all to do with punishment.
Though it was no less a claiming.

This time, it was a seduction.

Pleasure and dark promise.

He took her face in his hands, and he tasted her as he'd wanted
at last. He teased her lips until she sighed, melting against him, and
opened to let him in.

He kissed her and he kissed her, until all that fury, all that need,
hummed there between them. He kissed her, losing himself in the
sheer wonder of her taste and the way that sweet-sea scent of hers
teased at him, as if she was bewitching him despite his best efforts
to seize control.

Cenzo kissed her like a man drowning, and she met each thrust of his tongue, then moved closer as if she was as greedy as he was.

As if she knew how much he wanted her and wanted him, too, with that very same intensity.

And there were so many things he wanted to do with her. But kissing her felt like a gift, like sheer magic, and for once in his life, Cenzo lost track of his own ulterior motives. His own grand plan.

There was only her taste. Her heat.

Her hair, which he gripped with his hands, and the way she pressed against him.

There was only Josselyn. His wife.

He kissed her again and again, and then he shifted, meaning to lift her in his arms—

But she pushed away from him, enough to brace herself against his chest. He found his hands on her upper arms.

"I agreed to marry you," she panted out at him, her lips faintly swollen and her brown eyes wild. "I refuse to be a pawn in your game."

"You can be any piece on the board that you like," he replied, trying to gather himself. "But it will still be my board, Josselyn."

He let her go, lifting up his hands theatrically. "By all means, little wife. Run and hide if that makes you feel more powerful."

He kept his hands in the air, his mock surrender, and laughed at her as he stepped back.

Because he'd forgotten, entirely, that they stood on those narrow stairs.

It was his own mocking laughter that stayed with him as he fell, a seeming slow-motion slide backward when his foot encountered only air. He saw her face as the world fell out from beneath him.

Don't miss
The Sicilian's Forgotten Wife
available September 2021 wherever
Harlequin Presents books and ebooks are sold.

Harlequin.com

Love Harlequin romance?

DISCOVER.

Be the first to find out about promotions, news and exclusive content!

[f] Facebook.com/HarlequinBooks

[y] Twitter.com/HarlequinBooks

[o] Instagram.com/HarlequinBooks

[p] Pinterest.com/HarlequinBooks

[You Tube] YouTube.com/HarlequinBooks

ReaderService.com

EXPLORE.

Sign up for the Harlequin e-newsletter and download a free book from any series at **TryHarlequin.com**

CONNECT.

Join our Harlequin community to share your thoughts and connect with other romance readers!
Facebook.com/groups/HarlequinConnection

HSOCIAL2021